10p

Dancing Horses

The only grand thing Francisco Javier possessed was his name. He was a destitute child, wandering a Spain still recovering from the Civil War, but when his friend Pepe was killed on the Casares' bull ranch he was taken in, fed and given a job looking after the old grey mare, Gaviota.

That was a new beginning, for Francisco Javier found he liked horses. Indeed he came to adore the golden colt, Gavilán, the colt who hated people and grew wilder day by day. Francisco Javier was sure that if only *he* were Gavilán's rider he could tame the colt, and together they could become stars of rejoneo, the art of mounted bullfighting.

It was an impossible dream, and the story of how it came true, of how the destitute boy found a home and a future, and the wild horse found a master, is a moving and powerful story. Helen Griffiths writes about animals and their relationship with people uncompromisingly, and with a clear-sighted conviction.

Readers of THE LAST SUMMER, a recent book by Helen Griffiths, will remember Gaviota.

HELEN GRIFFITHS

Dancing Horses

Hutchinson
London Melbourne Sydney Auckland Johannesburg

Hutchinson Junior Books Ltd

An imprint of the Hutchinson Publishing Group

3 Fitzroy Square, London W1P 6JD

Hutchinson Group (Australia) Pty Ltd
30–32 Cremorne Street, Richmond South, Victoria 3121
PO Box 151, Broadway, New South Wales 2007

Hutchinson Group (NZ) Ltd
32–34 View Road, PO Box 40-086, Glenfield, Auckland 10

Hutchinson Group (SA) (Pty) Ltd
PO Box 337, Bergvlei 2012, South Africa

First published 1981
© Helen Griffiths 1981

Set in Baskerville by Bookens, Saffron Walden, Essex

Printed in Great Britain by
The Anchor Press Ltd and bound by
Wm Brendon & Son Ltd
both of Tiptree, Essex

British Library Cataloguing in Publication Data

Griffiths, Helen
Dancing horses.
I. Title
823'.914[J]   PZ7

ISBN 0-09-146160-X

*A note on some of the Spanish words
used in this book*

The word 'señorito' has various meanings. In general terms it can be translated as 'young gentleman'. As used by servants, and particularly in the south of Spain, it means 'master', regardless of the master's age. It is also used contemptuously, a señorito being a person of leisure, anyone arrogant, or a snob.

'Rejoneo' refers to equestrian bullfighting, performed by a 'rejoneador'. It takes its name from the spear used to kill the bull, the 'rejón'.

A 'torero' is a professional bullfighter of any category.

'Gavilán' means 'sparrowhawk'.

1

The biggest thing about the boy was his name – Francisco Javier. It was long and pretentious and everybody automatically called him Paco or Paquito, the common nickname for all Franciscos. But his name was all he had, his one memory of a time quite beyond recall in every other respect, so he wouldn't surrender it. He clung to it stubbornly as the only thing that belonged to him, that distinguished him from everyone else.

A woman had always called him by that name. He knew she was his mother. He remembered her voice although he couldn't recall her face at all and had even given up making imaginary pictures of her. He had lost her somewhere, before awareness began, in a nightmare of noise and panic, and all that remained was the way she had called him.

'*Francisco Javier!*' her strident voice, impossible to ignore, stretching out the last syllable in a long, echoing demand as he played in the street, unwilling to leave his games.

It was surely the longest, most important sounding name in all the world and he was certain his mother had never called him Paco. But now no one called him Francisco Javier unless they were teasing him, wanting to make him cry – no one until he met Pepe.

Pepe had picked him up on the road after he had run away from the orphanage. He had run away because he was tired of being hungry and because he was old enough to look after himself. When there was nothing to eat Father

7

Ambrosio prayed and, while he prayed, hunger didn't seem to matter. It was only afterwards, trying to sleep on his bed of rags in the burnt-out church – the magic of the beautiful-sounding words and their hypnotic rhythm broken – that his hunger would return in all its agony.

He ran away on the day he discovered the road that went to Madrid, its very emptiness amid the yellow plains tempting him to adventure. Who could tell what might lie beyond the horizon, or in the capital itself? Then he met Pepe, travelling in the opposite direction – going south – and because Pepe took him seriously and always used his proper name Francisco Javier stayed with him, although he was hungrier than he had been at the orphanage and his bed was always in the fields and ditches.

Pepe had great plans for making his fortune as a torero.

'It's the only way for a poor man to become rich, unless he's a politician,' Pepe told him, and Francisco Javier believed him because the only famous people he knew of – the ones who had their photos plastered on café walls or on the streets – were one or the other. He preferred the idea of being a torero, because of their glittering costumes of silver and gold and their dangerous livelihood. The politicians wore white shirts and ties, and their eyes were cold and lifeless.

Pepe was a few years older than his companion, at sixteen almost a man in Francisco Javier's eyes. His father had been killed in the war and he had run away from home because no one wanted him to be a torero. He had the look of all the famous toreros; eyes made big and tragic by the gauntness of his hunger-ridden face; and the proud, disdainful stance with which he taunted his bull – Francisco Javier charging at full speed with a sharp-pointed stick in each hand – was a straight copy of all the posters either of them had ever seen.

His cape was an old, grey blanket stolen from home

8

which kept him warm at night and in which his few possessions were rolled. Francisco Javier had no possessions to add to this roll but as the future torero's personal assistant – with the grand title of 'Sword Handler' – it was his duty to look after it and carry it along the lonely, dusty roads.

For a long time Francisco Javier believed that Pepe would never find a real bull to cape, nor even a heifer. Few villages along their way were able to afford to buy or rent an animal with which to liven their annual fiestas and those that could had usually already contracted lads willing to risk their lives and didn't care much for strangers, unless they had a real cape or a proper costume, however tattered.

Instead, Francisco Javier obligingly played bull every day, charging at Pepe's outstretched blanket with as much artfulness as he could muster on an 'often empty stomach. He took his part so seriously that his friend's teasing, tempting cape became a torment to him. He longed for the day when, instead of rushing head down, straight through it – eyes momentarily blinded by its dark and heavy clinging – his skull would crash against Pepe's body and bring him to the ground.

It was hard work playing bull and it was even painful when Pepe practised the kill, using a stick which he would dig between his friend's shoulder-blades, sometimes too enthusiastically.

Pepe said they must go to Sevilla, the breeding ground for toreros. There he would meet all sorts of people who could introduce him to others who would know somebody who could help him. And so they set out for Sevilla, begging their food, stealing it, learning – at times painfully – what could and couldn't be eaten of the wild plants and fruits in the countryside.

As they went along they talked. Francisco Javier was always insatiably eager to hear about Pepe's family and adventures but when Pepe returned the questions there was nothing the younger boy could tell him. Before he had joined Father Ambrosio's flock of hungry war orphans, he had lived like an abandoned dog, and his memories of those days were so vague as to be almost non-existent.

He remembered a day when he was a lot smaller, when he had hidden in a field with other people because the soldiers were coming. The grass was long and buzzing with insects. It made him sneeze and he had been terribly frightened because everyone else was frightened. But this memory could have been a dream, a nightmare. He didn't really know. There had been so much hunger that half his life had been lived in a daze, with nothing to recall that had any meaning, except the sound of his mother's voice shouting his name.

One day they found themselves beside a ranch where fighting bulls were bred. At hardly any distance from the roadside, and beyond walls topped with barbed wire, a herd of some thirty beasts placidly grazed. The sun glistened on their hides and when Pepe called to them in a low, coaxing voice several looked in his direction, big jaws moving slowly, ears expressing curiosity.

Nothing in their actions just then showed that these were the fiercest of wild beasts, bred to attack at the slightest provocation and to endure the hardest punishment. They were far bigger than Francisco Javier had imagined, immense creatures whose horn span was surely as wide as his outstretched arms.

'Tonight one of those bulls will be mine,' Pepe suddenly said with such quiet determination that Francisco Javier felt a thrill of fear for him.

Well into the night the two friends pulled themselves up on the wall, scraped under the wire and dropped into the pasture. Francisco Javier planted his bare foot on a thistle and let out a sharp cry, which Pepe just as quickly silenced with a hiss. The bulls had moved further away downhill, towards some trees by a stream, and the moon had turned them into harmless, hornless shadows.

They half ran, half slunk across the pasture towards the trees, making a wide detour of the bulls which hadn't become aware of them. Francisco Javier's heart thumped with fear. The bulls looked bigger than ever now. Only his admiration for Pepe kept him a short pace behind.

They stayed among the trees for a little while and Francisco Javier could smell the sweet, sickly aroma of the animals they had travelled so far to encounter. He could hear them chewing the cud. One stood slightly apart from the rest, a very black shadow against the pale sky.

'That one's mine,' Pepe breathed.

'He's very big,' Francisco Javier couldn't help remarking. Just then he wouldn't have minded if Pepe suddenly decided he didn't want to be a torero after all.

Pepe spread his blanket cape as he had done so many times with his little human bull about to confront him. He made a few practice passes, fingers tightly clenched in the cloth, then fiercely demanded, 'Swear by your mother that you won't move from here.'

Francisco Javier couldn't see his face in the shadows but he could sense the fear that was in him, as well as the excitement. He nodded, too frightened to speak.

Without letting go of the blanket, Pepe crossed himself with his thumb. Then, suddenly, he ran in an arc towards the lone bull, a frail figure in the moonlight. The bull didn't know what to make of him and at first he just looked, big ears thrust forward, wet muzzle glistening. Then he lowered his head with a threatening thrust, bunching his huge shoulder muscles, but otherwise planted where he was.

'Come on, bull,' Pepe almost whispered caressingly, although to the watching boy it sounded like a shout, so strained was every nerve.

11

Pepe gave a slight flick to the blanket. The bull shook his head once more and started pawing up dust and grass. Then he charged, his ponderous bulk suddenly swift, graceful and deadly.

Francisco Javier instinctively shut his eyes, feeling sick as the hooves thundered through him. When he opened them again Pepe was still standing there, handling his blanket with confidence as the bull made a lightning turn and charged with a thrusting right horn straight for his body. At the last moment, though, the bull followed the blanket and passed miraculously beneath Pepe's outstretched arm, the cloth stroking along his back.

Again the bull turned but this time he paused, his attention caught by the herd not far away. He looked once more at the elusive, moonlight shadow then, dismissing it contemptuously, trotted off to his companions.

'What was it like? What was it like?' Francisco Javier shouted wildly, forgetting all caution as Pepe came back to him. He was so glad that Pepe was still alive and there was a pain of love and pride in his heart.

'Did it look good?' Pepe answered, unable just then to tell Francisco Javier what it was like because still he didn't know himself. Not till the next day did he say it was the most powerful and wonderful thing he had ever experienced.

They laughed and joked and pushed each other around as they recrossed the pasture and got back over the wall, and very soon afterwards both were asleep, exhausted by their emotions, unaware of the moonlight on their faces.

Francisco Javier didn't know it was illegal to cape bulls in the pastures. He knew nothing about bulls at all, beyond what he learned from Pepe, and Pepe hadn't told him that the bullfight was based on the principle that the bull has never been confronted by a dismounted man with a cape. A bull needs only twenty minutes to learn to distinguish a man from a cape. After that, he doesn't chase the cape any more. His horns seek out only the man.

Neither had Pepe told him what might happen if they were caught by the herdsmen whose job it was to protect the bulls from intruders such as themselves. One day, however, he found out. This was before they reached Sevilla. They were well into bull-breeding country and Pepe had tried his skill in various pastures. On a good night he might get a dozen passes out of a game bull, all the time working him closer and closer to his body, but nights like this were rare.

It was after such an occasion, when for the first time Pepe had consciously let the bull go rather than lost him, that the herdsmen caught them. They were a long way from any cover and the moon was particularly bright. They heard galloping hooves and suddenly they were surrounded by guards who, with shouts of rage, threw themselves off their horses and set to beating them until their yells of pain echoed across the pastures. For days afterwards tears were never very far from Francisco Javier's eyes. Every part of him hurt.

They came to Sevilla without encountering any more bulls or herdsmen. It was Francisco Javier's first experience of a large city. He wandered open-mouthed up and down the narrow streets and wide avenues, gaping at buildings six or eight storeys high, entranced by glimpses of flower-filled patios behind iron grilles. He was bewildered by the traffic, both horse-drawn and motorized; astonished by the trams; and impressed by the biggest river he had ever seen with its ocean-going ships.

Even Pepe was left speechless when at last they found themselves gazing at the famous bullring, La Maestranza. They wandered round and round the several narrow streets that led to its different entrances, Pepe dreaming out loud of the day when he would come here with his team to fight the greatest bulls, and Francisco Javier believing him.

2

They spent the winter in the city. Pepe found work for them both, cleaning out stables. They slept in the stables and ate in the kitchen of the tavern to which the stables belonged, their wage being one meal a day and any small tip a generous horseman or muleteer might offer them.

Every day they hung about La Maestranza, sometimes at the main entrance before the big iron gates, sometimes at the back where the booking office was. Although there were no bullfights in winter it was the natural meeting place for anyone connected, however slightly, with the profession. There were gypsies with decrepit nags for sale, impresarios looking for a promising torero to manage, failed toreros desperately looking for some kind of employment when the season started, and many hangers-on unable to resist the feel in their blood that anything to do with the bulls inspired.

One day someone told Pepe that a breeder called Casares was about to hold a bravery test for his young heifers. 'He'll often let a lad like yourself show what he can do,' this man said, and so the night before the testing was to take place Pepe and Francisco Javier walked the thirty kilometres to the Casares ranch, full of hope and excitement.

They arrived at about three o'clock in the morning, weary and shivering with cold, huddled together with Pepe's blanket across their shoulders. Moonlight shone on the arched entrance set back from the road. There was the

Casares brand, well-known all over the country. They could make out buildings and trees at a distance and, beyond them, hills blending into the darkness. There were no lights and they were afraid to approach any closer before dawn, so they curled up together at the base of the entrance and fell asleep.

They were woken by people in carriages, people on horseback, people on foot and people in cars making for the Casares house. The testing of the heifers on this occasion was especially important, as the two boys were to discover when they mingled, uninvited, among the many guests and listened to a dozen different conversations.

Don Ramón Casares had lost most of his bulls at the beginning of the war, six years earlier, when they were slaughtered by local anarchists, and this was the first testing to be held since then. The bulls were tested by horsemen in the pastures but the heifers had to undergo a more rigorous trial, for the bull gets its bravery from its dam and only the bravest and most fearless would be kept for breeding.

These youngsters were the two-year-old offspring of stock bought at high prices from all over the country. Don Ramón had a reputation to keep up from times gone by and everyone there that day, including experts from all over the region, was eager to see how well he had chosen and crossed his new seed stock.

But how to recognize Don Ramón among the crowd between the house and tentadero – a small bullring with stockyards and stables behind – to ask his permission to make a few passes with one of the heifers? Eventually someone pointed him out – 'That fat gentleman with the big cigar' – and for nearly an hour Pepe and Francisco Javier moved within arm's reach of Don Ramón, who could change Pepe's life at a word, without catching his eye.

Everyone wanted to be near Don Ramón that day, complimenting him, joking with him, making promises,

15

begging favours, reminding him who they were. He was surrounded by a group of landowners and breeders as important as himself who shielded him from all but the people he actually wanted to talk to.

Several times Pepe began, 'Please, Don Ramón . . .' but someone always pushed in front of him or shouldered him aside without even noticing him.

The day went by. They didn't go hungry because food had been splendidly laid out for everybody and there was pale gold wine by the cask, but Pepe couldn't even get into the tentadero as a spectator, let alone as a participant. They heard the cheers and applause and snatched breaths which told them that Don Ramón's heifers were living up to expectation, but they saw nothing.

Pepe's thin face was tight with fury.

'I'm going to find myself a bull today if it's the last thing I do,' he muttered to Francisco Javier, eyes smouldering. 'If Don Ramón won't give me a chance, I'll take my own. Come on. Don't let's waste any more time here.'

Francisco Javier lingered just long enough to fill his shirt with bits left over from the feast laid out for the guests. To him food was more important than the bulls and he had never seen so much in one place at one time. Pepe was angry but he had enjoyed himself, seeing all these rich people dressed with such splendour for a special occasion, and their sleek, matching carriage horses decorated with bells and ribbons. He had never known that such people and such horses existed.

That night, squatting in one of Don Ramón's pastures, he filled his stomach with food from Don Ramón's tables and jabbered contentedly to Pepe about all he had seen and felt. Pepe wasn't hungry and he pushed Francisco Javier's offerings away. He still burned with resentment and all his companion could get from him was muttered remarks about 'señoritos'.

16

By chance that night they found the pasture where Don Ramón's best seed bull grazed. He was an enormous animal, all of six hundred kilos, as innocent as he was fierce and easily lured by the two boys dancing just out of his reach, calling him, taunting him, irritating him. Pepe got three perfect passes out of him before Francisco Javier, watching awe-struck from a distance, became aware of the riders bearing down on them from whom there was no escape.

This time, however, there was no immediate beating. Their hands were tied and running, tripping, cutting their feet on stones and thorns, they were dragged behind the horses to the overseer's house.

Señor Miguel's temper wasn't improved by being woken up at four in the morning and every shouted question or demand was accompanied by a blow from the walking stick he had taken from a hook on the kitchen wall. He cursed and hit them, and hit and cursed them, and then said he would turn them over to the civil guard who would probably beat them again.

'Put them in the pigsty for now,' he shouted to the men who had brought them in, 'and make sure they don't escape.'

In the darkness of the shuttered sty, overcome by the smell and their pain, they were unable to console each other. Francisco Javier tried to think of all the beautiful people and horses he had seen that day, but it was very hard when all he had to look forward to was another beating and all his body burned and ached.

Pepe said, 'It's their fault, if they won't give me a chance,' so Francisco Javier knew he was still angry.

The civil guard didn't come and the overseer wasn't so angry later that day because it wasn't often that his men managed to catch lads playing the bulls in the pastures. He was very pleased at having two culprits to show to Don

Ramón's youngest son who came round about mid-day, accompanied by one of his sisters. Their beautiful grey horses snorted and cavorted with disgust at the two boys, smelling of pig, who were dragged out in front of them.

'And what kind of pigs are these?' said the young man with a laugh. Black-haired, dark-eyed, he looked no older than Pepe, but how sleek he was, how handsome!

'This one here,' replied Señor Miguel, poking Pepe in the ribs with his walking stick and making him wince, 'was caping Rencoroso when we caught him. The other was just watching.'

'Do you know my father's herdsmen could shoot you for doing that?' the young señorito demanded haughtily of Pepe, making his horse push into him and nearly knocking him over.

'What shall I do with them, Señorito Lolo?' the overseer asked.

'Lock them up in the pigsty again. It seems to suit them. We'll see what my father decides.' Turning to his sister, he exclaimed, 'Let's go, Mari-Angeles. There's a terrible stink around here.'

It seemed to Francisco Javier that, before urging her horse after her brother's, the girl flung a compassionate glance in their direction as they were shoved back into the pigsty with the help of Señor Miguel's walking stick. But when he mentioned this Pepe gave a scornful laugh and said that his head had been turned by yesterday's dreams, or perhaps by a whack on the skull.

They spent two more nights and days in Señor Miguel's pigsty, eating what they could wrest from the sow who lived there, for the rest of the time trying to keep out of her way. Every now and then she rushed at one or the other of them, trying to flatten them against the wall. Her squeals were deafening, her smell suffocating, and both boys were utterly

18

crushed by the misery of their situation. They hammered on the door for attention and shouted until they were exhausted, but the overseer was deaf to their pleas.

'I only obey orders,' he told them, laughing at their desperation. 'I was told to lock you up. No one's told me to let you go. Without Don Ramón's orders . . . .' The overseer shrugged. He cared nothing for their suffering. He didn't even think about it.

'Suppose Don Ramón's forgotten all about us?' Francisco Javier fearfully asked Pepe in the dark.

Pepe didn't answer.

On the third day they heard hoofbeats, then voices, and Señor Miguel opened the door of the pigsty and called them out. Though he blinked in the sunlight Francisco Javier immediately recognized Mari-Angeles, mounted on the same grey horse. There was a look of shocked concern in her eyes as she turned to the young man on the tall, dark horse beside her.

'You see? I wasn't exaggerating. We should have come sooner. They've been here three days.'

'It's not my fault, señorita,' Señor Miguel began. 'You heard what your brother said. He told me to lock them up. I would have let them go sooner but you know how your father feels about these lads.'

'You were only doing your job, Miguel,' the young man stopped him. 'However, I think they've learned their lesson. Isn't that so?' he demanded of Pepe, directing a very cold glance at him.

His hat was worn at such an angle that only when he moved his head to look at Pepe did Francisco Javier see the gouged and puckered scar that disfigured his face between left cheek and temple. He noticed, too, that the left sleeve of his jacket was empty.

Pepe was sullenly silent. He didn't even look up and Francisco Javier knew that the anger that had begun in him

19

on the day of the testing still wasn't quelled.

'And what about you, boy?' the young man said to Francisco Javier. 'You're a bit young to start this kind of life, aren't you? You'll end up in gaol, the pair of you.'

'I only wanted a chance at the testing,' Pepe suddenly burst out, flinging up his head in impulsive anger. 'But Don Ramón only gives the chances to señoritos like yourself.'

'My father has nothing to do with vagabonds,' came the icy reply. 'If you really cared about the bulls you wouldn't be caping them illegally. One day, if you ever get to the bullring, you may lose your life because of a bull that's been caped in the pastures by someone like you.'

He turned his horse in a gesture of dismissal. 'Let them go,' he told the overseer, adding with a backward glance at them, 'There's a river north of here. You could both do with a good scrubbing. When you're clean, keep going north.'

'And good luck!' called Mari-Angeles as they cantered away.

They bathed in the river, flinching and groaning even though the cold water soothed their many bruises. Then they spread their tatty clothes out on the bank in the spring sunshine and, shivering from time to time, waited for them to dry. Francisco Javier saw that Pepe's face was dark with bitterness.

'They have no right to treat us like that. No right,' he kept muttering.

'Perhaps we shouldn't cape the bulls any more,' suggested Francisco Javier.

'You don't have to do anything you don't want to. Go back to the stables in Sevilla. Maybe you'll have a job there for the next forty years.'

'I don't want to be a stable boy. I want to be rich.'

Pepe gave a scornful grunt. 'Then sit here and dream. That's as near as you'll ever get to it. I'll go back to the bulls by myself.'

'But not here, Pepe. Please,' Francisco Javier begged him. 'I don't want to go back to that pigsty if they catch us again.'

'They won't catch us. We'll be more careful. And we'll play the cows this time. That's not so bad. We'll go tonight because they won't expect us.' He laughed out loud, his voice hard. 'They'll never expect us tonight.'

'I don't want to,' Francisco Javier said sullenly. 'You're crazy.'

'I don't need you. I managed on my own before.'

'You haven't got a cape now. We lost the blanket,' Francisco Javier reminded him hopefully.

'I'll use my shirt.'

'Please don't go, Pepe. Perhaps there won't be enough moon.'

Pepe answered with an oath.

The moon was on the wane but gave enough light for Pepe's purpose. They went back together and found a herd of young cows who looked no size at all compared to the bull Pepe had caped a few nights before. It was bitterly cold, with a wind that blew icily from the sierra. Francisco Javier didn't know if his teeth chattered with cold or fear. He knew it was only Pepe's hurt pride and stubbornness that made him insist on going ahead instead of leaving things for a better occasion.

They walked for ages before they found the cows and then had a very difficult job trying to separate one from the rest. The animals kept bunching up and moving away, wanting to know nothing of the boys who teased them, and then when one did break loose she swept after them with such vicious energy that both had to run for their lives. Luckily, she was confused by having two enemies instead of one, and while she hesitated they gave her the slip.

But Pepe came back to her, full of angry bravado, struggling with the shirt in his hands as it flapped in the wind. Francisco Javier saw the cow race straight towards him, head lowered, and the next moment Pepe was under her hooves, only visible on the dark ground because of the shirt that was somehow tangled round him.

Without thinking, Francisco Javier ran towards the cow who was wheeling round for a second charge, screaming to distract her and give Pepe a chance to scramble away. But she went for Pepe again, butting him in the stomach as he half staggered to his feet, and he went down a second time. The cow kept on course, back to the herd, and the two boys were alone.

Pepe tried to get up but collapsed with a groan. Francisco Javier stared at him, frozen with dread. There was no blood but he looked deathly in the cold moonlight and began to moan for his mother. Francisco Javier wrapped Pepe's shirt round him then tore off his own to add what little comfort he could, and the tears fell hot from his eyes as he leaned over the only person he had ever loved, listening to his groans.

He had never known so long a night and he wished that the guards would come because he was so afraid for Pepe who couldn't get up and was lost in pain. He considered running for help but it might take hours to find someone – and suppose they started beating him instead of listening to his plea for help? Besides, he couldn't bear to leave Pepe alone.

After a time Pepe stopped groaning and writhing, much to his companion's relief. He was unconscious. Francisco Javier fell asleep in spite of the cold and his dread, and he dreamed of Mari-Angeles, a graceful figure astride a tall, dark horse, with a hint of golden hair beneath the grey, Cordoban hat. Suddenly she was standing over him, shaking him hard, and her face was different, severe . . . .

In fact, it was her brother – the older one – and Francisco Javier dragged himself out of his stupor to realize that he wasn't dreaming any more. The sun was over the fields; he was stiff with cold; Pepe was still lying there, unmoving; and the señorito was talking to him as though from a great distance. He seemed further away than the girl in his dream and his words meant nothing. He had the odd sensation of being outside himself.

He saw himself struggle into the saddle of the señorito's horse; saw himself take the cotton rug that was unstrapped from the saddle and wrap it round his naked shoulders; saw himself on the horse, cantering across the pasture, sharing the saddle with the young man who had only one arm, but because he felt nothing, nothing was real.

3

When things started being real again Francisco Javier found himself in a huge bed with soft pillows and mattress, pure white linen and a colourful bedspread. This was more like a dream than reality because he had no memory of having been in a proper bed in all his life. The room – with its big silver crucifix on one wall and a framed coloured print of a beautiful Virgin with tears on her cheeks on another – was enormous and furnished in the same generous proportions as the bed, all of which made him feel very small and scared.

Where was he? He didn't know, or couldn't remember.

Just then the big door opened and Mari-Angeles came in, accompanied by a servant carrying a tray of breakfast things. At first he didn't recognize the señorita who looked entirely different in a flowery, short-sleeved dress, and then he remembered! Everything came back to him, up to his last memory of Pepe.

'Oh, you're awake! I was hoping you would be,' she exclaimed.

Her accompanying smile somewhat assuaged the sudden bleakness in his heart. As he sat up in the bed she laughed, her whole face alight with amusement.

'Those are my brother's pyjamas. You look lost in them,' she explained.

He discovered very quickly that the Señorita María de los Angeles, Don Ramón's youngest daughter, intended to enjoy her role of nurse. She rolled up the sleeves of the voluminous pyjamas, knotted a serviette round his neck, pulled up a chair and forcibly fed him. There was a sugary bun which she broke into the large bowl of milky coffee and pushed into his mouth in big spoonfuls, hardly giving him time to swallow. She talked vivaciously, both to him and the servant, waving the spoon from time to time to give emphasis to her words.

'I learned to do this with my sister's baby,' she announced, laughing, thrusting a bit more soggy bun at him. 'He never wants to eat. But you must be hungry. Do you know you've slept for more than twenty-four hours? We didn't know what to do with you so we put you in here. And the doctor came and said to let you sleep, that you'd be all right, and the civil guards came and wanted to talk to you but I wouldn't let them wake you up. And my father shouted and said it was quite ridiculous, that you ought to be in gaol, but I persuaded him to let you stay here till you're better. I'm looking after you and you can't go till I say so.'

When at last Francisco Javier could get a word in, the coffee and bun finished and the señorita silent for a moment, he said, 'And Pepe? What about him?'

'Was he your brother?' For a moment she looked serious.

Francisco Javier shook his head.

'The civil guards want to ask you about him. They want to know his name and where he came from.'

'His name's Pepe and he's always been with me. He's going to be a torero and I'm going to be his sword handler.'

'He's not going to be a torero now,' Mari-Angeles told him. 'He died.' As he just stared at her she went on, 'Cry if you want to. I shan't mind.'

He dropped his gaze but he didn't cry. Some things hurt too much for tears. Besides, hadn't he already known and cried, alone in the pasture? That little burst of hope was only self-deception, defiance of the unbearable.

Mari-Angeles told the servant to take the breakfast things

away then reminded him, 'The civil guards still want to see you. But don't be scared. They only want to ask some questions. I expect they'll shout but I won't let them hurt you. I'll stay with you if you want. Do you?'

He nodded, without meeting her eyes, and was glad of her protection when the interrogation began. He remembered little of that interview. Terror overwhelmed him as first Don Ramón and then the civil guards shouted threats and questions at him. When they eventually went away Mari-Angeles stayed by the bed and talked to him, struck by his helplessness.

'Don't you have any family at all?' she asked unbelievingly. 'My eldest brother was killed in the war but I've still got two brothers and three sisters. They're all older than me. All my sisters are married and two of them have got babies. And then there's aunts and uncles and cousins and so on, and my grandparents, in Sevilla . . . . Haven't you got anyone?'

Francisco Javier shook his head. Without realizing it, she was making things worse for him. He stared down at the coloured bedspread feeling somehow ashamed of his solitary condition, guilty even. He didn't want to talk, but she persisted.

'Do you want to tell me about your friend?'

Again the brusque head-shake.

'What will you do now? Where will you go?'

He shrugged his shoulders inside the floppy, striped pyjamas, hurting too badly to talk.

'You could stay here,' she said. 'I could ask my father to give you a job.'

'He won't want to,' he managed to mutter because she was expecting him to say something.

'I'll persuade him. Half the time he doesn't know who works here and who doesn't. Besides, he won't be angry for long. It's just that the bulls mean so much to him. You must promise not to go near them again.'

26

'I hate them,' he cried with fierce pain.

'Then that's settled. I'm going to find you some clothes – yours are awful – and when I come back I promise I'll have a job for you.'

Francisco Javier didn't really believe her until she returned with an armful of clothes that fitted fairly well and were certainly better than anything he was used to. There was even a pair of well-scuffed, rope-soled sandals, a bit big but not noticeably so when he'd tied them up.

Mari-Angeles did up the shirt buttons and straightened the jacket. Then she stood him in front of the wardrobe mirror.

'What do you think of yourself?' she asked.

He had never seen himself in a mirror and it was like looking at a stranger, though not entirely because the face and figure he saw was so similar to those of all the boys he had known at the orphanage: thin, sunken-eyed, with sticking-out ears and unruly brown hair, dressed in other people's unwanted clothes. He didn't like what he saw – this reflection of charity – and turned away without answering.

'Do you know anything about horses?' the señorita then asked.

'I've worked in a stable but . . . .' He shrugged.

'You're not scared of them? You like them?'

'I don't know if I like them, but I'm not scared.'

There was enough spirit in his answer to please her and she went on, 'They're wonderful creatures and we have one in particular that needs looking after. She's an old mare – ever so old – and she always has a boy just to take care of her. All you have to do is feed and groom her and follow her around, see that she doesn't hurt herself or get into mischief.'

'Follow her around?'

'Yes. You see, she's rather special. She used to belong to one of my aunts. This was years ago. She's at least a hundred

in horse's years now. She was never kept in a stall, like the
other horses, and – '

'Why not?' He was curious now.

'Because my aunt treated her as if she were human. She
was a rejoneadora, my aunt. She fought bulls from
horseback and Gaviota – that's the mare I'm telling you
about – was her best mount. Both of them used to be
famous, while I was only a baby, and my father's favourite
horse, Azabache – a black stallion – was her first son.
Gaviota wasn't here when the war started or she would have
been slaughtered like the others. She's the only one left from
the old days, which is why my father cares so much about
her.'

She went on, 'He got two more good foals out of her,
since the war, in spite of her age – a colt and a filly. There
never was a mare quite like her, I can tell you. She wanders
about wherever she pleases. My father wouldn't mind if she
came into the house, but she can't get up the stairs.'

'Hasn't she got a boy now?'

'She did have but my brother Lolo didn't like him, so he's
gone.'

'He doesn't like me, either.'

'If you keep out of his way he won't even remember you
exist. There's hundreds of kids here like you. You can eat in
the kitchen with the cook's children and she'll find you
somewhere to sleep. My father said so.'

'Don Ramón?' It seemed impossible to Francisco Javier.

'He's not so terrible, really. Only when someone upsets
his horses or his bulls. If you look after Gaviota well he'll
probably forgive you. Let's see if we can find her now. At
this time of day she's usually downstairs, looking for
something to eat.'

She rushed him along a corridor full of tall, shaded windows
and down a staircase that doubled in width as it joined with

one from the opposite corridor and descended to the courtyard. Out in the bright sunlight, Francisco Javier was as much dazed by the patio with its riotous profusion of flowers and greenery clambering and dangling everywhere over white-washed arches as by the shining marbled floors, mosaic walls, dark portraits and heavy lamps he had passed upstairs.

Flowers hung in baskets from the arches, twined round the balconies above them, lined the walls in an endless row of plant pots and even decorated the central well and the water trough in one corner. Hanging among the flowers were small cages with canaries and linnets who challenged and answered each other in loud bursts of song. There were a number of people about who stopped whatever they were doing when Francisco Javier appeared beside Mari-Angeles to stare at him in frank curiosity.

Within the arches, under the house and half in shadows, were stalls where chained horses turned their heads with pricked ears to watch them.

'Jubiloso, Princesa, El Moro, Manzanares, Teniente and . . . as I thought, Gaviota!' sang out Mari-Angeles as she passed each animal and came to the end stall where a grey mare busily mouthed up the last few grains of barley someone had poured into the manger for her. When this was done she turned towards the two watching humans, thrusting her well-shaped but grizzled head into Mari-Angeles' outstretched hands. She wasn't chained, like the rest.

So this was the famous Gaviota, so special and so close to Don Ramón's heart that Francisco Javier was to have the particular job of being her devoted slave!

Dark hair dappled her silvery white coat, her legs were black, her mane and tail steel-grey. There were deep age sockets above her inquisitive eyes and the passing years had stiffened her joints and weakened her sinews. Once, perhaps, she had been beautiful but now she was like an old

29

woman whose youth was hardly even a memory. She blew through her nostrils in greeting and rubbed her head against Mari-Angeles while examining Francisco Javier from the corner of one eye.

'You see, she'll use you as a rubbing post just as soon as she knows you. This stall is hers but she's never chained up. She likes to be here at night, with the others, but she'd go berserk if she were tied. You can't even put a head-collar on her. If you do, she stands like a mule and refuses to move. Juan's in charge of the horses here and he'll tell you how to look after her. Most of the time all you have to do is follow her around and try to keep her out of the grain store. She's the greediest horse I know. Aren't you, my darling?'

Francisco Javier put out his hand to stroke her dark nose. It was softer than anything he had ever touched. She nuzzled his jacket then turned back to the manger to see if there was any barley corn she'd overlooked.

'Come on. I'll show you her daughter, Princesa. She's a three-year-old. My brother's going to start training her soon. He's out with Gavilán just now – that's Gaviota's son, the first colt born here since the war. He's a four-year-old and a bit of a handful.'

Princesa looked almost exactly like her dam, a dapple grey with black points and steel-grey mane and tail. Her head was less refined than Gaviota's, who had a dished Arab face, but her expression was equally gentle. She whickered eagerly, small ears pricked, and Mari-Angeles began to stroke her. The grey in the next stall shook his head up and down, rattling his chain and squealing.

'That's Teniente,' laughed Mari-Angeles. 'He's mine and he hates me to make a fuss of any of the others. All right, my darling,' she soothed him, stroking her fingers down his long, scarred nose and kissing his muzzle. 'You know I love you best.'

Mari-Angeles couldn't leave the horses without offering a

30

word, a caress or even a kiss to each one and then she took Francisco Javier down an obscure passageway, where several small children ran about noisily, to introduce him to and leave him with the cook, Domitila, her nursing role and her interest at an end.

The cook had four sons, the eldest no more than nine years old but already helping her husband, a herdsman, in the horse pastures. She was thin and sharp, talkative, and from the first day she treated Francisco Javier as she treated all her boys, shouting a lot, whacking them from time to time, but keeping them generously supplied with Don Ramón's food.

Domitila had no intention of calling him Francisco Javier. 'As far as I'm concerned your name's Paco and if you don't like it you'll have to lump it. Whoever heard of such a name? Your father must have been crazy. Why, even the señoritos don't have names like that!'

'I shan't take any notice of you if you call me Paco,' he protested stubbornly, protecting the only thing that was his.

'Then you won't get anything to eat!' was her triumphant reply. She was used to winning every argument and when words failed her a frying pan or cooking pot would do instead.

He didn't get any lunch because before she put the soup plate in front of him she asked him his name and he defiantly replied, 'Francisco Javier', which made all the boys laugh. At supper-time, some ten hours after Mari-Angeles had spoon-fed him with the coffee-soaked bun, she asked him again. There was garlic soup and a huge dish of cabbage and chick-peas on the table from which everyone helped themselves. Domitila didn't offer Francisco Javier any soup and when she saw him stretching towards the central dish she slammed a wooden spoon down on his fingers, making him yell.

'What's your name?' she asked him again, black eyes

teasing but unrepentant, and all the boys echoed her, even the smallest who was hardly three.

By then he was feeling too tired, hungry and miserable to care. 'Paco,' he said, exchanging his pride for a bowlful of soup and a stomach full of chick-peas. You could feel very hungry on a diet of pride.

After eating he went to the patio for a last look at Gaviota. She'd already had her supper but he brought her two handfuls of barley, just to make friends with her. The old mare munched slowly, her eyes half closed, and standing beside her Francisco Javier felt less lonely than he had all day.

'I wish I were a horse,' he told her, and just then he really meant it.

From what he had seen that day the horses got kisses, caresses and loving attention, but he didn't even know where Pepe was lying that night.

There was an old striped palliasse behind the straw and sacks of grain in the feedstore where he could sleep. There were no pillows or fine linen, just a sheet made from flour sacks and a horse blanket that smelled like Gaviota and kept him warm. He and Pepe had sometimes talked about having a mattress. One of the first things they were going to have when Pepe made money from the bulls was a real bed to sleep in. They had talked a lot about such things as they huddled on the ground under one blanket, keeping each other warm.

Suddenly Francisco Javier was crying as he'd never cried in his life but not only because he'd lost Pepe. He cried for the mother he couldn't remember; the father, brothers and sisters he'd lost or never had; the home life he'd never known; and because for the first time he was truly aware of the loneliness of having no one to care about and no one to care for him.

4

Francisco Javier stayed at the Casares ranch because there was nowhere else to go and at least he had the security of two meals a day and a bowl of hot chicory for breakfast.

It took him a little while to get to know all the people who lived in the recesses of Don Ramón's sprawling house, behind stables and kitchen and storerooms. Only the upper storey was occupied by the Casares family. The ground floor was a dark warren with passages that led to rooms without windows, where whole families of dependants lived and where Don Ramón and his family hardly ever ventured.

There were several lads to look after the dozen horses kept in the patio. They had all been born in the house and looked on Francisco Javier as an intruder. The head groom, Señor Juan, had been born in the house, too, before its present master.

The gentlest of men with horses, he was more of a tyrant than Don Ramón and much more feared by everyone under him. He expected the patio to look at all times as though no horse ever clattered over its cobbles and he himself was always as impeccably dressed as any señorito in short jacket, close-fitting calf-length trousers and Cordoban hat, typical of the region.

Although he ate each day with the cook's family and had a place of his own in Don Ramón's overflowing establishment, Francisco Javier still had his loneliness to struggle with. Nobody cared about him in spite of the questions they first

plagued him with. If anything, they were suspicious of him –
a possible favourite thrust among them by Mari-Angeles.
He had to fight his own battles again and console himself, or
go without consolation, and it was very hard in the
beginning.

He cried himself to sleep under the horse blanket until
one night he must have run out of tears because, although
his heart still ached for Pepe, he could cry no more. In the
daytime, with the bustle and noise and Gaviota, he was
cheerful enough.

Don Ramón came down every morning after breakfast
and his grey Andalusian stallion, Jubiloso, had to be ready
for him in spotless condition. Sometimes, before riding off
to inspect his bulls and cows and horses in the pastures,
Don Ramón would look at old Gaviota and say a few words
to her, but he never said anything to Francisco Javier. He
probably didn't remember who he was.

Lolo – called Señorito Manuel by all but the oldest
dependants who were entitled to some familiarity – hadn't
forgotten him, though. Whenever he happened to notice
him – which wasn't very often because, like his father, he
only noticed the people he wanted to see – he would throw
some reminder to him of Señor Miguel's pigsty.

The younger señorito and his sister were often together,
racing the horses, challenging each other to make their
mounts do something ever more difficult. Señor Juan
would mutter under his breath about them when they
returned horses, sweating or jaded, that had to be walked
for an hour before they could be safely left in their stalls.

Both were superbly confident riders and they spent half
the day on horseback. Francisco Javier often watched them
and his respect for the horses he knew so little about grew
into wonder that they could be taught to do such marvellous
things. In particular, he liked watching Mari-Angeles. The
only girls he had ever seen in his pillar-to-post life reflected

the poverty of his own existence. Mari-Angeles of the golden hair was a luxury whose high-spirited vitality added brightness to his day, especially if she happened to smile at him as she sometimes did.

At times Don Ramón joined them with Jubiloso to prove that, in spite of his weight and greying hair, he and his stallion could do anything they could and perhaps better. They were displays of unashamed vainglory, their mounts' extravagant and haughty actions an extension of themselves. But José-Ramón, now the eldest son, never joined them and Francisco Javier soon learned that the aloof and humourless señorito had been so shaken and hurt by the war that he had been at odds with his family ever since.

Francisco Javier was naturally curious about the person who had first of all saved him from Señor Miguel's pigsty and then taken him so painlessly away from Pepe. Remy, who looked after his horse Lucero, seemed to like him. He said José-Ramón was a much better rider than anyone in the family but Francisco Javier didn't believe him, any more than he believed Remy's assertion that the señorito's left arm still hurt him.

'How can you feel something you haven't got?' he argued scornfully, determined not to be made a fool of this time. He was always being teased.

Remy shrugged. 'I don't know, but it's true. He doesn't often get mad but one day he was really going at me for next to nothing. I must have looked dead scared or surprised, or something, because he suddenly apologized and said it was because his arm was giving him hell. So there.'

Francisco Javier couldn't imagine a señorito apologizing for yelling at a stable boy, so he assumed Remy was trying to make him look green again and questioned the cook instead. Domitila prided herself on being an authority on the whole family's history. Hadn't she lived in the house for thirty-five years and overheard every squabble?

And so she told him about Eduardo, less than a year older than José-Ramón, as handsome and wild as Lolo was now, and who had been everyone's favourite.

'Eduardo and José-Ramón did everything together. Like inseparable twins they were,' she sighed, 'getting in and out of every kind of scrape together. You wouldn't think it, to see him now. So serious. Mind you, José-Ramón always used his head, even when he was little – which is more than anyone else here ever does – so Don Ramón never worried about what they got up to. But volunteering for the war was too much, even for him.'

She stopped and shook her head sadly, remembering.

'If you'd have seen Don Ramón in those days! He was so broken up about everything – the bulls, the horses, his brother being murdered. He just sat on the steps in the patio and cried. We all saw him.'

She paused, still impressed by the memory, then went on, 'He raved like a madman at José-Ramón when they enlisted. He said, "You could have stopped your brother. You've got more sense than he has," and for a long time he wouldn't forgive him. And then, in the very last big battle of the war, at the Ebro, Eduardo was killed and José-Ramón . . . . Well, you already know. The two sides were killing each other there for three or four months, first in the heat and then in the snow, as if they'd never tire of it. So many of them died.'

She said this with an ache in her voice.

'The señorito didn't come home for a long time and when he did he was still in a bad way. Don Ramón didn't know how to treat him. I think he couldn't help being angry with him because it hurt him so much. And as for his mother . . . I can tell you, this was a sad house for a long time. Things have never been the same since those days,' she finished.

*

Soon Francisco Javier could groom Gaviota as well as any boy there, and because he spent so much time in her company, he talked to her as once he used to chatter to Pepe. She liked this and he didn't need to follow her about any more because she took to trailing him everywhere. She even waited for him outside the grain store early each morning, and about the only time she ever broke into a trot was when she tried to beat him back to the stall where he gave her the morning feed by the handful.

If he overslept, as he sometimes did, she would start whinnying and banging at the door with her hoof, which would start the other horses off, too. At first this annoyed Francisco Javier but when he realized it was as much because Gaviota was eager to see him as because she wanted her breakfast, he didn't mind so much.

He knew she was pleased to see him because she would push him about with her nose, tickling him, making short blowing sounds as if she was talking to him.

Señor Juan happened to be watching one day and he said appreciatively, 'She's taken a real fancy to you. That's a good sign because horses don't take to everybody, especially that madam. She's had half a dozen lads to look after her and I haven't seen her care about any of them like she cares for you.'

This was high praise indeed. Señor Juan was far better at cursing and cuffing than paying compliments and he was obviously impressed. Whether he would have been as pleased to know that Gaviota was getting at least twice her daily barley ration, which had certainly encouraged their good relationship in the first place, Francisco Javier neither knew nor cared.

Remy achieved his desire to become a herdsman in the bull pastures and because Francisco Javier was usually up before anyone else, thanks to Gaviota, and also because Señor Juan felt like promoting him, he was given the job of looking after Lucero as well as Gaviota, though he was only shrimp-size and the gelding was all of sixteen hands.

'I can manage him,' insisted Francisco Javier eagerly, proud of the promotion and not meaning to be done out of it through any physical shortcomings. 'I'll stretch, Señor Juan. You'll see.'

'The most important thing you have to remember,' Señor Juan impressed upon him, 'is to have the horse ready before the señorito comes down. He doesn't like to be reminded that he's no longer able to tack up a horse by himself, and you won't get very far in this place if you annoy the señoritos. You look after Lucero well, without neglecting Gaviota, and there might be better things in store for you.'

Because the señorito was always around before anyone else – sometimes even before Gaviota had eaten her breakfast – Francisco Javier got up extra early the first morning Lucero was in his charge. He'd hardly slept all night, afraid of not waking in time, and dawn was just breaking. Gaviota was lying down in her stall but she was soon on all fours at the sound of his footsteps, looking somewhat startled by this reversal of custom.

While Lucero was groomed she stood beside his stall, whickering jealously and nipping his rump, although she'd had her breakfast. Francisco Javier had to drive her away several times. It was hard enough to work on such a big horse, without having him jumping about nervously, trying to avoid Gaviota.

He led the gelding out to tack him up and Gaviota bit Lucero's neck. In the end he had to give her a second barley ration to get her out of the way. In spite of this, Lucero was ready long before the señorito wanted him and Francisco Javier felt very pleased with himself.

When José-Ramón appeared he made a thorough inspection of Lucero, aware that he had a new groom. He picked up each hoof in turn, examined the bridle and curb

38

chain and checked the girth. Francisco Javier, by the drinking trough with Gaviota, watched apprehensively, wanting so much to have done everything right.

'Come over here,' suddenly demanded the señorito, hardly looking at him, and he hurried to obey, nervously biting his lip.

'You tacked up Lucero this morning, I believe,' he said, both tone and expression inscrutable.

Francisco Javier nodded. José-Ramón grasped the pommel, gave one tug and the whole thing slipped sideways, stopped only by the crupper. The gelding began to kick frantically until José-Ramón took hold of the reins and soothed him with soft words.

'Well, get the girth undone, boy, and saddle him properly,' he said impatiently because Francisco Javier was frozen to the spot by the disaster.

He could hardly undo the buckles, so much did his fingers tremble under the señorito's stern gaze, but at last the saddle was in the right place and the girth good and tight. It had taken him at least five minutes, which had seemed like an hour, and he knew it was far too long.

'Is this the first time you've saddled a horse?' José-Ramón asked him.

He nodded miserably without looking up.

'Did no one tell you that most horses have a habit of blowing themselves up just as soon as they feel the saddle on their backs? You think you've got the girth as tight as it will go but if you look again ten minutes later you can tighten it another couple of holes at least. Next time, remember to recheck the girth.'

That was all he said before riding away but still Francisco Javier felt sick at heart. When Señor Juan heard of it he'd probably box his ears and never trust him again. He would have liked to take Gaviota as far as the river and keep out of the head groom's way all day, but he knew he'd have to be around to take charge of Lucero when the señorito returned and he didn't dare risk a second reprimand.

To his surprise Señor Juan didn't get to hear about the loose girth. José-Ramón must have voiced no complaint. On the contrary. At the end of the first week Señor Juan said to him, 'The señorito says he's pleased with the way you look after Lucero and wants you to stay with him. I think you're going to be a good lad with horses,' he added of his own accord.

5

Now that Francisco Javier had a proper job to do in the stables, instead of just being Gaviota's nursemaid as the other boys called him, he found himself getting more and more interested in the horses. The ones he cared most about, apart from Lucero and Gaviota, were Princesa and Gavilán because they were Gaviota's offspring. He hoped that one day he would be able to look after both these horses, especially when he knew that Santiago, who cared for Gavilán, hated the chestnut and was longing to swap him for another horse.

The boys often talked among themselves about the horses and all of them agreed that Gavilán was the worst of any they had ever had to deal with.

'That horse hates people,' Santiago told them one day and he pulled off his shirt to show them the bruises on his arms and shoulders where Gavilán had bitten him. 'You're welcome to him just as soon as Señor Juan gives the word,' he said to Francisco Javier, 'but I think you're crazy to want him.'

'Just because Gaviota's so soft with you, it doesn't mean her son's going to be the same,' said Antonio who looked after Jubiloso and Teniente but dreamed only of being a torero. 'Look at Lolo – ' They all giggled at his scornful use of the familiar nickname. 'He can manage any horse in the stable. Right?' he demanded, insisting on their reluctant agreement. 'But he's getting nowhere with Gavilán.'

All this talk about the chestnut colt filled Francisco Javier with more and more desire to look after him. He already thought Gavilán was the most beautiful horse in the world because of his colouring. He had seen every kind of grey horse and roan; and bays ranging from mahogany to black; but this mixture of sunset and gold, unbroken by any white markings, was unique.

His head was like Gaviota's, dished and refined, with large, brilliant eyes and small ears. Señor Juan said he was three-quarters Arab which accounted both for his colouring and his light conformation. He wasn't very tall, about fourteen and a half hands which made him seem quite small beside Lucero, but he was just the right height for someone no bigger than Francisco Javier.

He tried to make friends with him as he had so easily with all the other horses. He would stand in their stalls and talk to them, rubbing their ears and their jaws, but none of this worked with Gavilán. He couldn't even get close to him in the stall because the chestnut colt had a habit of shooting round his head with snapping teeth and an expression evil enough to frighten off anybody less persistent than he was. Never had any horse been so unresponsive to overtures of friendship.

Francisco Javier didn't give in easily, however. Barley corn had eased his way into Gaviota's heart. Perhaps it would have the same effect on Gavilán. Every morning, before getting Lucero ready for José-Ramón, he would take the chestnut a handful of corn and in return Gavilán tried to crush him against the side of the stall, or lunged at him with wickedly bared teeth. He wasn't yet brave enough to ignore such attacks but neither would he give up trying. One day, surely, Gavilán would understand that he didn't want to hurt him.

'What do you want with that colt?' Señor Juan asked him,

aware of how hard he was trying to gain Gavilán's confidence.

'Why's he so bad?'

'Well . . . .' Señor Juan paused to arrange his thoughts. 'There's some horses that need gentle persuasion and some that have to be forced into everything with a lot of discipline. Most of them come in the middle, a bit of persuasion, a bit of force, but from what I can see, Gavilán is very much like his mother. She's the gentlest, cleverest horse that ever lived and she was lucky enough to fall into the hands of someone as gentle and clever as herself. That was Don Ramón's sister, the Señorita Angeles. I expect you've heard talk of her. There was never such a woman with horses. She had inborn power over them, telepathic perhaps.'

'Telepathic?' asked Francisco Javier, stumped by the word.

'It means being able to communicate a thought or feeling without using words, just by thinking or feeling it strongly enough. If you watch, you'll see that horses and other animals do it all the time, though they use sounds and signs as well. But they don't need to talk like human beings, and that keeps them out of trouble.'

'And Gavilán . . . ?'

'Now if ever a horse needed telepathy, that one does, but the Señorito Manuel knows as much about telepathy as a gate post. When that colt first came into the patio he was as soft as butter. Highly strung, perhaps; a bit wild and full of beans, but nothing I haven't seen in many a colt before him.'

'Then why's he like he is?'

'That's not for me to say.' Señor Juan had long ago learned to keep his opinions to himself. 'All I'll say is that he'll never be another Gaviota unless he finds another Señorita Angeles. She could have calmed him down and

43

turned him into a dove. But that colt is half crazy already and if you've got any sense you'll keep well away from him.'

A chance for him to look after Gavilán didn't come until Easter when all the biggest events of the year began, starting with the Holy Week processions, continuing with the most important horse and cattle fair of the region, accompanied by a dozen bullfights, and finishing with the traditional pilgrimage to the distant province of Huelva. No one could imagine any of these events taking place without horses, so when Don Ramón moved the family to the city to be on hand for all the celebrating – and, so it was said, to spend a few obligatory weeks with his wife who preferred to live in Sevilla, near her married daughters – most of the horses went, too.

Señor Juan and all the stable boys, but for Santiago and Francisco Javier, were to spend the next few weeks in Sevilla. These two had to stay behind to look after Gavilán, Princesa and Gaviota. Santiago was very sullen but Francisco Javier didn't care. His memories of Sevilla were too closely tied up with Pepe for him to want to go there.

Before going away Señor Juan gave Santiago and Francisco Javier a long, much repeated lecture on how to look after the three horses left behind, reminding them of their responsibility. He said Princesa and Gavilán were to be walked each day and then turned out separately in the corrals for a few hours and that he expected to see them in perfect health and tip-top condition when he returned.

'And watch that Gavilán,' he warned Santiago. 'Don't let him get away from you or you'll never catch him again.'

Señor Juan had hardly left the patio when Santiago made a deal with Francisco Javier. 'You look after the horses and I'll do everything else.'

This suited Francisco Javier very well for there were no jobs he hated more than mucking out and cleaning the patio. He could spend all day with the horses, and perhaps by the time Señor Juan came back he would be getting on so well with Gavilán that he might be allowed to take him over from Santiago permanently. In his enthusiasm he forgot that Gavilán still wouldn't let him enter the stall without threats and intimidation.

The first morning it took all his courage to ignore the champing teeth, the rolling eyes, the stamping, kicking legs, just to give him his feed. He skipped grooming him altogether, and walking him round the patio, and didn't even think of taking him over to the corrals. He bluffed his way through Santiago's malicious curiosity, too proud to admit defeat so soon.

On the second day it was just as bad, the colt snorting and squealing and working himself into a sweat, and he knew that somehow he had to stop being afraid of him. Until he did they could never be friends. Unless he did he wouldn't even be able to step in his stall again.

He took Gaviota down to the river, wanting to keep out of Santiago's way, and spent several hours beneath the trees, mostly thinking about Gavilán, trying to work out what was wrong with him. To use Señor Juan's favourite expression, most of the horses were like butter, so why should Gavilán be so different? Why was he so mean?

Gaviota wandered up to him as he lay back on the warm earth, shielding his eyes from the sun that filtered through the leaves above him. She sniffed and snorted round him for a while, tickling his ears with short breaths, and he stretched up an arm lazily to scratch her jaw, which she always loved.

'Why isn't Gavilán like you and Princesa?' he asked her. 'Why did you have such a son?'

He remembered what Señor Juan had said about some horses needing telepathy and Gavilán being perhaps one of them. He had no idea how to use telepathy but already he was sure of one thing. Gavilán knew he was afraid. Would

45

pretending he wasn't be telepathy and, more important still, would it deceive the colt? It would be better not to be afraid at all but that wasn't easy. Pepe had always been afraid when he faced a bull but he'd never run away. Perhaps he could pretend he was Pepe. He had to do something because, more than anything, he wanted the colt one day to push his beautiful head against him, as Gaviota did, waiting to be scratched on the jaw.

Knowing how much Gaviota liked to be talked to, and never at a loss for words, Francisco Javier spent most of the afternoon talking to Gavilán. He didn't go into the stall but leaned just out of reach against the partition. Gavilán began his usual restless dance from side to side, snorting and shaking his head, sweating, but after a while he grew tired of so much movement and drew himself up by the manger. Belligerently he watched with one white-rimmed eye, ears laid back, whole body tense; but also, in spite of himself, he listened.

Francisco Javier went on talking and Gavilán began to relax. The whiteness went from his eyes and his ears came forward. He rubbed his nose against his knee and sniffed his empty manger, blowing disappointedly. Then he took the weight off one hind leg and stretched out his neck to doze.

'Looks like I've talked you to sleep,' Francisco Javier remarked with a grin. He'd almost talked himself to sleep, too, but he was satisfied because never had Gavilán been so quiet with a person near.

He was very much tempted to go into the stall, to run his hands down the shining neck and breast, but he knew he would spoil things if he did. He suddenly understood that Gavilán needed time, space, that the stall was a prison for him as well as a home; that he was still very much a creature of the open country, unready for discipline. He didn't know how he realized this – unless it was the telepathy Señor Juan talked about – but he felt it to be true.

What would the chestnut colt do now if he was set free? Would he come back at feeding time, as Gaviota always did, or would he never come back at all as Señor Juan had grimly warned? He didn't dare make the experiment but determined to do the next best thing, which was to turn him loose in the corral and leave him there all the time Señor Juan was away. He'd pretend to Santiago that he couldn't catch him – perhaps he wouldn't be able to, anyway – and he'd worry about what Señor Juan would have to say when the time came.

He turned him out that very night. Gavilán bit his chest as he clipped the leadrope to his headcollar but at least he didn't try to run away once they were outside the house. Francisco Javier was very grateful for this because, terrified of losing him, he had wound the leadrope twice round his hand, aware even as he did so of the risk he ran of being dragged as far as Gavilán felt like taking him.

Gavilán pranced sideways, tossing his head up and down, snorting fiercely, and Francisco Javier talked to him the whole time, as much to calm himself as the colt. It was late and for once Gaviota wasn't interested in following him, too set in her elderly ways to care for a night excursion. He was grateful for this too because he didn't want her jealously attacking Gavilán.

Once safely in the corral he unbuckled the headcollar and watched with pleasure as Gavilán bucked and kicked all the way round, spooking at his own shadow. He showed Francisco Javier all his paces in the moonlight, from a gay walk to a tail-high gallop and the flowing, exaggerated movements were so beautiful, so free, that the boy felt a pain in his heart as he watched.

Gavilán halted and stared straight at him, ears pricked, eyes brilliant in the moonlight, body quivering with contained power. He lifted his off foreleg high and pawed

47

the ground three times, swirled a complete circle, then came back to face him again, very still for a moment before trotting off into the shadows with tossing head and loud snorts.

Francisco Javier grinned and called out to him, 'All right, all right. I know you're a señorito but you've also got to be my friend.'

The colt ignored him and didn't notice when at last he went away. It was hard to sleep that night with the vision of such power and beauty engraved upon his mind.

6

After only a few days he knew that Gavilán was different. His tenseness was gone. He would come up to see what the boy had brought in his pockets, empty his palms of barley in the gentlest way and stand quietly to be groomed, almost pushing his head into the collar. Francisco Javier talked to him all the time and Santiago came to watch in amazement, unable to understand how the colt that made his life such a misery could suddenly be so gentle.

'Well, you can keep him,' he said. 'Señor Juan will listen to you now and I don't want him back. What have you done to him?'

Francisco Javier didn't try to explain. Although he was now half accepted by the others, there was none he cared enough for to share any of his innermost thoughts or feelings. If Pepe had been around he would have told him how he dreamed of Gavilán, how he loved him. He would even have tried to explain how he felt when he watched him or groomed him, making sunglow in his coat of fire. Pepe, whose passion for the bulls was like his own feeling for Gavilán, would have understood.

Just as Pepe could never have been satisfied with being only a spectator in the bullring, so was he beginning to realize that forever being Gavilán's groom wasn't enough. Every day as he stood so close to the chestnut colt, seeing and feeling the power that was in him, the urge to mount him increased until it became an obsession. He didn't know the first thing about riding, except what he had learned from watching Lolo and Mari-Angeles. This wasn't much because they were such effortless riders that the horses seemed to obey them by magic rather than by any physical command.

One night, after hearing the children who played round the house called into supper, he went to the corral, sure there'd be no one around. He slipped a headcollar on Gavilán and mounted from the water trough, hoping the colt wouldn't be aware of his pounding heart and be frightened by it. Gavilán put his ears back and tensed up a little but that was all.

He eased himself forward, taking care not to let his dangling legs touch the colt's flanks. Gavilán was as still as a statue, except for his ears which kept turning to listen to him, and gradually Francisco Javier relaxed. He couldn't have described the sensation that sitting there with such power within his grasp gave him, but it was very special, very profound.

He drew his hand caressingly down the colt's mane, along his neck, growing in confidence, certain that Gavilán had accepted him, was in tune with him. Then, with an irrepressible smile, he sat up straight, put his free hand on his right hip, tilted an imaginary hat after the style of a señorito, and urged Gavilán into movement with a click of his tongue.

The colt obeyed but without any particular impulsion, not knowing what his rider – lost in a dream of wonderful possibilities – wanted of him. Very soon he halted, tossing his head up and down, and Francisco Javier just sat there, warm with happiness.

Several times he rode Gavilán in the darkness, mounting from the trough, growing more confident as he began to get the measure of the colt's movements and respond to them. Then he began riding him after grooming him each morning, giving no commands, a relaxed, day-dreaming passenger who sometimes fell off when Gavilán made abrupt, unexpected movements. After every ride there was a handful of grain.

Gaviota waited patiently outside the corral, resigned to sharing him. She never went off on her own now and dozed nearly all day long, lower lip dangling like an old woman's.

Santiago found out what Francisco Javier was up to.

'Señor Juan would skin you alive if he knew,' he warned, 'and don't tell me what Lolo would say!'

'I'm not doing any harm and, anyway, I'll stop when they come back.'

'Why don't you ride him properly? Saddle him? I'll get the tack if you like,' he offered, glad of any escape from the daily routine.

The proposition was too tempting to be ignored, even though Francisco Javier struggled against it for a while. Santiago's encouragement was all he needed to make him feel that it wasn't such a bad thing to do, but the daredevil look in the other boy's eyes made him cautious.

'You won't tell anybody, will you?' he demanded. 'Promise?'

'Not if you let me have a go, too.'

He didn't want this at all but there was no way of refusing without making an enemy of Santiago.

'Perhaps we ought not to . . .' he began but Santiago laughed scornfully and said, 'Are you chicken? I tell you, no one will know.'

He ran off but as soon as he returned with saddle and bridle Gavilán began to get excited, dancing round with flattened ears and making throaty noises. Neither words nor hands could calm him and suddenly he reared up, yanked the leadrope from Francisco Javier's hand and made straight for the open gate at a gallop, almost knocking Santiago flying as he swept past him.

51

'Idiot!' Francisco Javier screamed at Santiago, recovering from momentary paralysis, and he dashed after the colt feeling sick with dread.

Gavilán had no intention of stopping. He was off towards the pastures, tail high, rope trailing, and the two boys looked at each other, panic-stricken.

'We shan't catch him,' prophesied Santiago gloomily. 'What shall we do?'

'I'll follow him,' was Francisco Javier's desperate reply. 'He's not scared of me. I'll get some barley and maybe he'll come to me. You stay here in case he comes back, but don't let anyone know unless we have to.'

The only other time he had known such sick fear in his stomach was when Pepe had been hit by the cow. The sun was hot and his throat was dry with fear and dust as he alternated between running and walking, trying to keep up a fast pace until his breath came too hard and painfully. Gaviota followed and there was something comforting about the sound of her hooves behind him. But he couldn't stop thinking of all the things that might happen to Gavilán. He was such a crazy horse, after all.

He might go non-stop through a barbed wire fence, or get the rope entangled in his legs. Supposing he got into one of the bull pastures? Would they go for him? The best thing that could happen, which would still be bad for Francisco Javier, was that one of the herdsmen might manage to stop him and bring him back.

He hurried on, rubbing his sweat-filled eyes on his dirty sleeve, thinking of every awful possibility, and he forgot about Gaviota who every now and then stopped and whickered to him in a complaining way.

To his immense and incredible relief he found Gavilán by the river, tearing at a luxuriant patch of grass and wild flowers. The colt looked up at his approach and whinnied a greeting to which Gaviota replied. He looked unhurt and very calm, but would he allow himself to be caught or would he dash off again as soon as his freedom was threatened?

Francisco Javier wasn't taking any chances. He knew he couldn't follow any further. He was too exhausted and almost doubled up with stitch. He could see that Gavilán was already getting nervous so he decided to pretend no interest in him at all.

He went further along the river bank and knelt down to wash his hot and sticky face after drinking a few mouthfuls of water, and then he settled back in the shade of a holly oak, making sure that Gavilán could see him. He talked to Gaviota and gave her a few grains of the barley he had brought for the colt. Soon he saw that Gavilán was highly interested and not a little jealous.

'Come on then,' he called to him. 'There's some for you, too. I brought it for you. But you've got to come here for it. I'm not going over there.'

He gave Gaviota one grain at a time, which made her rather cross, but he couldn't afford to let her have it all. However, her impatient stampings intensified Gavilán's curiosity. Suddenly he made up his mind and trotted up to the pair of them with sharply pricked ears, squealing for his share. Gaviota tried to bite him, which put him off for a moment, but he saw the barley in the boy's outstretched hand and reached out for it.

Francisco Javier let him eat, using all the insults he knew in a most caressing tone before gently taking hold of the leadrope. Gavilán made no objection and when eventually they started back he followed quietly enough, in step with Gaviota.

Francisco Javier tried to puzzle out what had frightened or upset Gavilán. Was it Santiago, or was it the saddle and bridle? He could perhaps find out by saddling him himself to see what happened, but for a while he wanted to make no experiments. For a few days he didn't even mount Gavilán again, too shaken by what had happened.

However, the colt was as consenting as ever when he slipped onto his back again. He decided to ride him only early in the morning or just before supper, when no one was around, and he was doing this one night when he suddenly became aware of being watched. Looking round he saw José-Ramón and Lucero. How long had they been there?

He wanted the earth to open up and swallow him just then as he froze on Gavilán's back, not knowing whether to stay where he was or jump down. He couldn't tell what the señorito was thinking and could hardly see his face anyway. All he said was, 'Lucero's tired and hungry. Come and see to him,' and then moved away.

Francisco Javier hung about in the corral for as long as he dared, hoping that José-Ramón would just leave Lucero in his stall and go away before he appeared, but he couldn't stay away too long in case he was waiting for him. His heart sank even further when he saw man and horse by the water trough in the patio, Lucero dribbling a last unhurried mouthful, and he hung back, biting his lip.

'How long have you been riding that horse?' José-Ramón asked, still not giving anything away by his tone of voice and not bothering to look at him, busy loosening Lucero's girth.

Used to Señor Juan's bullying shouts and lightning cuffs, he didn't know how to respond to the señorito's imperturbable manner, how best to defend himself – not that he had any defence this time.

'Only a little while,' he managed to reply, forcing himself to draw closer.

'Did Señor Juan give you permission?'

'No . . . .'

'When the cat's away, eh?'

Francisco Javier was close enough now to take hold of the reins from the other side of Lucero so he didn't have to meet

54

the señorito's eyes. In his heart he couldn't accept José-Ramón's accusation. He hadn't been taking advantage of Señor Juan's absence just because he was away and yet, in a way, he had. It was too difficult to try to explain so he remained silent.

'Well?' José-Ramón continued with relentless calm, moving Lucero's head so that now Francisco Javier couldn't escape his gaze without hanging his head.

'Please, señorito, forgive me. I won't do it again, I promise,' he pleaded, very scared, not knowing what his punishment might be but dreading being forced to leave the horses that filled the emptiness of his life.

'Is that the truth?'

'Yes, sir. Really. I promise,' he repeated, meeting José-Ramón's dispassionate grey eyes with desperate hopefulness.

'Then you're not like your friend? I warned him to keep away from the bulls and he took no notice.'

'He didn't promise, señorito. He would never have made such a promise.'

'But you would. You don't feel as much for horses as he felt for the bulls, do you?'

Francisco Javier couldn't follow this line of questioning. He felt trapped, sure that José-Ramón was deliberately taunting him by reminding him of Pepe, as heartless as his brother after all. He couldn't think of anything to say, crushed and stung.

'Take Lucero. It's more than thirty kilometres from Sevilla and it's been a hot day. Feed him well.'

He had hoped the señorito would leave him then; suspend sentence till the morrow or Señor Juan's return; but he hung about and watched while Lucero was attended to. Now Francisco Javier knew how a mouse must feel, waiting for the cat to pounce!

He was clumsy in everything he did, tangling the chain, dropping the body brush twice and even managing to trip over his own feet. Lucero calmly champed away at his supper, and normally the sound would have been a comforting one. Lolo's threats would have been easier to bear than this silent intimidation which distracted him. When would he go away?

Suddenly José-Ramón said, 'Why do you ride him?'

Francisco Javier could hardly see his face in the dimness of the stall, especially with his hat pulled down as always, but surely there was genuine curiosity in his tone? Still scared of being trapped into saying the wrong thing, however, he only cautiously responded.

'It's just that Gavilán is – '

'Is what? Come on. All of a sudden you don't know how to talk!'

'He's special. I couldn't help wanting to ride him,' he defended himself impulsively, feeling even as he spoke the sensation that had first compelled him to climb on his back. If only he could make the señorito understand! His face burned.

'Do you ride any of the other horses? Princesa? Gaviota?'

'No, sir. Only Gavilán. But I won't do it again.'

'Damn you, don't keep saying that!' José-Ramón shouted at him. 'You're lying.'

'No, sir, I'm not. I – '

'Then you're just a layabout scoundrel like Santiago who gets up to all kinds of mischief when there's no one around.'

The señorito was tying him up in knots and desperation made him reckless. 'It's not true!' he cried. 'I love Gavilán. I understand him. I can do anything with him. That's why I ride him. I look at him and I can't help myself.'

The silence that followed seemed endless. Then José-Ramón said, 'You know nothing about horses and still less about riding but, if you promise to leave Gavilán alone – and keep your promise – I'll teach you to ride.'

Francisco Javier was stunned.

56

'The cat's eaten your tongue,' mocked José-Ramón.

'But why, señorito?' he stammered at last.

'Because you and that colt looked as though you belonged to each other. I'll see you tomorrow,' he said and strode away.

7

The sun was already high and hot, although it was still early in the day when Francisco Javier went to the yard behind the tentadero to look for the horse José-Ramón had said would be there for him. He had nothing to do with these horses, which were ridden and looked after by the herdsmen.

Few of them had the looks of the horses kept in the patio. They worked hard and there wasn't much time for special grooming and attention. Many of them had tails trimmed almost to the dock and no forelocks. They wore long leather fringes to protect their faces from flies and their noses were permanently scarred by the serreta, and the metal-toothed cavesson in common usage.

The only horse in the yard was a dark, dapple-grey gelding of fourteen hands or so, with gentle eyes that watched him curiously. He had time to spare so he took the horse into the stable, found some grooming tools and got to work to remove the dust from his coat. He talked to him at the same time, partly because like this the horse would get to know him and also because he liked talking anyway. The stable was cooler than the yard and he was in no hurry to be out in the sun. Gaviota came in and wandered from manger to manger, her soft muzzle nosing each one in search of any overlooked grain or chaff.

Francisco Javier worked slowly, trying to settle the nervousness that had attacked his stomach as soon as he got up that morning and still hadn't left him. He had hardly slept all night, worrying, and dreaming the kind of dreams that are only dreamt awake.

He had asked himself which horse he would ride. Would it be Lucero who was one of the handsomest horses in the patio with his satiny coat the colour of dark chocolate, his mane and tail a mass of black waves, his docile eyes full of intelligence? No. The señorito would never let him ride Lucero, or Gavilán, or any horse in the patio. Nothing, however, could stop him imagining himself with Gavilán, his rough clothes magically transformed as he took him through a series of brilliant airs such as were displayed by Lolo, Mari-Angeles and Don Ramón.

But then he thought of José-Ramón with his critical grey eyes and lofty expression, and the shattered side of his face that made Francisco Javier feel uncomfortable because he knew the señorito was sensitive about it and quickly put out if he thought anyone was staring at him. What kind of teacher would he be? Did the señorito really intend to show him how to ride or had he devised some form of punishment to scare him off? That morning he had seemed particularly intimidating when he reminded Francisco Javier to be in the tentadero by mid-day and told him about the horse.

Francisco Javier had felt so nervous that, in order to give himself confidence, he'd had to boast to Santiago about his forthcoming lesson. Santiago had called him a creep.

'Sucking up to the señoritos! And you've hardly been here a couple of months. Still, I might have known.'

'What do you mean?'

'Well, didn't the señorita get you a job here in the first place? I bet you're always running off to tell tales to her, and to Señor Juan. That's why he makes such a fuss of you.'

'He doesn't. It's not true!' he cried, hot with rage.

'No? First you were only to look after Gaviota. Then you took over Lucero and you've been creeping round José-

Ramón ever since, smarming up to him. Now it's Gavilán and Princesa – '

'You don't want to look after Gavilán. It was your idea because you're scared of him.'

'But if I'd have known then what you were up to . . .' went on Santiago with a sneer, ignoring the interruption. 'The others say you're a creep and they're right.'

'You're just jealous because Señor Juan's fed up with you and because you're scared,' accused Francisco Javier in turn.

They threw insults at each other until it developed into a competition to see who could come up with the most imaginative profanities and which, in spite of their animosity, they both enjoyed. Santiago won and even now, while he worked on the dapple-grey, Francisco Javier grinned as he thought over and repeated some of the richer phrases, determining to remember them for his own use.

In the tentadero the sun burnt down on the pale sand. There was no shade anywhere and Francisco Javier felt very much like a sardine in a frying pan. Time seemed endless to his fluttering nerves and the fear began to grow on him that perhaps he was there on a fool's errand after all, frying in the sun for his mortification and the señorito's amusement. But José-Ramón wasn't like Lolo, he told himself.

He looked round the neatly raked arena, with its protective wooden barrier scarred here and there by the horns of angry beasts, and with a pain in his heart he remembered how much Pepe had wanted to be here to show the skills he had learned so dangerously, recalling his fury and his bitterness because he had been denied. Pepe had died because he couldn't get inside this tentadero and now he himself was standing there, eyes hurting in the glare of sun and sand, at the whim of a señorito who would have been deaf that day to all petitioning.

Shaking off his memories, he decided to mount the dapple-grey. The saddle, with its high cantle and sheepskin padding, was extremely comfortable so it didn't bother him that his feet hardly reached the big box stirrups. He clicked his tongue and the horse obligingly began to move.

They circled the arena several times until, from lack of any consistent or intelligible orders, the horse stopped dead and refused to move any more. After that he just sat there and waited and when at last he heard Lucero's hoof-beats, he jumped out of the saddle too relieved to remember his nervousness.

'The first thing you're going to do,' began José-Ramón, 'is fetch another bridle like the one your horse is wearing. And be quick about it.'

Puzzled, and worried in case he had already done something wrong, Francisco Javier ran back with the bridle and gave it to the señorito, whose hand was free because he had knotted the reins and left them on Lucero's neck.

'You won't be needing stirrups so take them off,' was the next command. 'You can climb on from the burladero this morning. Later on you can teach yourself to mount without stirrups.'

He held the horse's reins while Francisco Javier pulled himself onto the nearest burladero – a shield of solid wood behind which a person could slip to escape pursuit – and tossed them to him once he was in the saddle. Then he pulled out a packet of cigarettes and lit one before saying, 'You like talking to horses, don't you?' and, in reply to Francisco Javier's cautious nod, 'Why?'

'Because . . . .' He stopped and shrugged, hardly knowing how to answer. He didn't think about it. He just did it. 'Because I do,' was all he could say, adding almost defensively, 'And they like it too.'

'That is so,' José-Ramón agreed with him, 'but not everybody realizes it. These horses of ours are very sensitive.

61

Docility and a willingness to please are bred into them. They understand us better than we understand them. So if they don't do what we ask of them, before resorting to punishment, we must ask ourselves if it's our fault. It usually is. Remember that. The horse you're riding, Mosca, knows far more than you do. Converse with him properly and he'll do anything you ask.'

'Converse?' queried Francisco Javier with a puzzled frown. It seemed an odd word to use.

'With your hands, heels, seat, back, every part of your body. Each slightest movement or weight change means something different, conveys a particular message. It takes a good horse a couple of years to learn most of the messages. A person needs much longer to get them right so don't presume any superiority.'

'Does that mean it'll take me years to learn to ride?' exclaimed Francisco Javier in dismay.

'It depends on what you mean by riding. After today you could take that horse all the way to Sevilla and back, though he'd probably be taking you. Horsemanship is something else. It implies a perfect understanding between horse and rider – a dialogue between friends, if you like. You've already established a conversation with Gavilán but, green as you both are, it won't get you anywhere. 'Hello. How's things? See you later.'

He dismissed this with a contemptuous wave of his hand but went on, 'However, it's a good start. No one else has got even that far with Gavilán. That's why we're here.'

Francisco Javier couldn't restrain a grin at the unexpected compliment. A moment later José-Ramón was thrusting the spare bridle at him.

'Put it on your leg, the left one, as if you were bridling a horse.'

Francisco Javier raised his eyebrows at this strange command.

'Imagine your leg is a horse's head. Place the bit across your shin, fasten the curb chain round your calf, hold up the headpiece and give me the reins.'

The bit had a deep port and shanks about six inches long. It was of the kind used for most of the horses. After some clumsiness, he had the port resting against his shin, kept in place by the chain fastened closely round his calf. He didn't even try to disguise his mystification as he handed the reins to José-Ramón, now close beside him but way above because Lucero was at least two hands taller than Mosca.

'This is lesson number one,' said José-Ramón, bending slightly as he gripped the reins about a foot away from the curb. 'Imagine that your leg is the horse's mouth.'

As he spoke he sharply tugged the reins backwards. Pain exploded in Francisco Javier's leg, forcing him to cry out as he toppled sideways out of the saddle in surprise.

'It's broken,' he howled in anguish, tearing the bridle off his leg, but with his back to the señorito so that he shouldn't see his involuntary tears.

'Come on. Get back on the horse,' José-Ramón heartlessly ordered him.

'I can't. I can't walk.'

'If you can't get on the horse I can't teach you anything,' came the reply with a touch of impatient scorn. 'It's up to you.'

Somehow Francisco Javier dragged himself onto the burladero again while José-Ramón manoeuvred Mosca into a suitable position. Once in the saddle, he dashed his sleeve across his face to clear it of tears then looked defiantly at José-Ramón, resentment throbbing as strongly as pain.

'My aunt did that to me when I was about five years old,' explained the señorito in reply to his look. 'I was the best horseman in all Andalusia then, knew everything there was to know. My favourite trick was stopping a galloping horse dead with a tug on the reins. I don't know how many times I

63

must have practised it until my aunt demonstrated what hell I was putting the poor animal through. Afterwards she taught me how to halt a horse properly. Lesson number one is to respect your horse's mouth.'

The lessons following that first one were hardly less severe and, in the beginning, almost as painful. All the work was done without stirrups and José-Ramón made no allowances for muscles unaccustomed to new demands. A lesson only ended when Francisco Javier had mastered something to the señorito's satisfaction, whether it took half an hour, an hour, or most of the morning. His sharp, dry commands pursued his pupil even while he slept.

'Loosen your legs!'

'Shorten the reins!'

'Straighten up!'

'Relax. Relax!'

Above all, 'Relax!'

'Until you stop tensing up you'll never get through to the horse. Your mind's not on him. It's on yourself.'

But was there anything more difficult than trying to relax every part of the body while, at the same time, needing to be consciously aware of each and every muscle in order to be able to use them unconsciously once they were under control? Once, when he felt he was really relaxing, José-Ramón shouted at him, 'I said relax, not fall asleep.'

The lessons were exhausting. His legs ached, his back was breaking, his shoulders felt crushed, yet still he had to see to Lucero and Mosca before he could drag himself to the kitchen for something to eat. He asked himself what he could have been doing right the night the señorito caught him riding Gavilán when, ever since then, all that he did was wrong.

After returning Mosca to the yard he would stop by Gavilán's corral to indulge in his one consolatory dream.

64

One day, when he was good enough, he would ride the beautiful chestnut and everyone would be taken aback at the sight of them. He didn't include José-Ramón in his 'everyone', certain by now that the señorito would find some imperfection in anything he did.

'There's no harmony between you and your horse,' was his main complaint. 'Poor Mosca is no more than a slave who is bound to carry you because he's too good-natured to rebel. Partnership is what you must achieve. Until you can tune into Mosca, who's only half as sensitive as a horse like Gavilán, you can't make any progress.'

And yet there was harmony between himself and the chestnut colt. He felt it as strongly as he felt the ache in his limbs. He still longed to straddle the glossy back he groomed every day and, in spite of his promise, he rode Gavilán again, sneaking out one afternoon when just about everyone in the house was fast asleep, except for a crying baby.

Gavilán snuffled up the grain he had brought him and made no fuss at all when he slipped across his back from the wall. As he sat there, soaking up the heat from the sun-coloured colt, intensely aware of the becalmed strength beneath him, all the ache went from his body. He was strangely aware of his own power, his own possibilities, and he suddenly understood what the señorito was trying to teach him through those endless exercises round and round the tentadero – entirely unconscious control through self-mastery.

Suddenly he and Mosca began to understand each other. There was a livelier feel to the horse's actions, an eagerness in the sharp movements of his ears, and half the weight seemed to have gone from Francisco Javier.

'Well, well!' exclaimed José-Ramón when they had completed hardly half a dozen turns round the tentadero.

He pursed his lips in an expression of surprised appreciation, and stared hard at Francisco Javier for a moment before searching for a cigarette. If he had any suspicion, any inkling about Gavilán – and for a heart-catching second it seemed that he might – the boy was determined to over-ride it with his disarming grin of satisfaction.

José-Ramón smoked in silence, head turned away, but Francisco Javier knew he was pleased. The heads of the two horses drooped side by side and Francisco Javier day-dreamed about Gavilán and himself.

These minutes of shared satisfaction were spoiled by the arrival of Santiago who called out, 'Señorito, Don Ramón's just arrived and he's sent me to tell you that he wants to talk to you.'

José-Ramón received this information with a muttered oath. He finished his cigarette before making a move, Santiago waiting at the gate for him.

Francisco Javier was intensely interested to know why Don Ramón had returned, obviously unexpectedly, and he was rather hasty in disposing of Mosca that morning. It was already rumoured that José-Ramón must have had a row with his family or he wouldn't have come back on his own before the fair was over. If Don Ramón was in a bad temper he would shout loudly enough for everyone to know what it was all about, and Francisco Javier was eager to be back in the patio before all the shouting was over so that not all the information he got would be second hand.

He ran back to the house, Gaviota trotting behind with little snorts of irritation, but strolled through the archway as nonchalantly as possible, a stable lad returning to his duties. But he soon gave up that pretence when he found everyone in the patio brazenly listening to Don Ramón's shouts echoing from the gallery upstairs.

He got only the tail end though, Don Ramón demanding unsuccessfully that his son return immediately to Sevilla, and he gave Santiago a scornful grin because now he knew where he'd picked up some of his swear-words.

People didn't even pretend not to have been listening when a defeated Don Ramón, hot-faced under a panama hat, stormed through them as if they didn't exist and slammed into his car. They stood round to watch him leave as he made a dreadful noise with the gears, and some even waved him off. Eventually they wandered back to their own affairs while still discussing the master's.

All Francisco Javier gathered was that it concerned the girl José-Ramón had been engaged to for some four years. Her father, Don Felix, was a breeder of bulls and a very close friend of Don Ramón's. She was supposed to ride with José-Ramón at the fair and his going away had offended everyone concerned. The señorito's excuse was that she didn't want to ride with him, anyway, and that several hours together on a horse under such circumstances would be intolerable for both of them.

This situation gave rise to all sorts of speculation but Francisco Javier was disappointed. Girls and engagements meant nothing to him. However, he was relieved to know that José-Ramón wasn't returning to Sevilla in spite of what people would say. He went to untack Lucero and rub him down.

'Creep,' Santiago hissed at him in passing, but he didn't care. Nothing could upset him that day.

Still, if he thought he had made a breakthrough and was ready to progress to more difficult things, José-Ramón wasn't of the same opinion. The next day it was as if he'd completely forgotten with what confidence Francisco Javier had taken Mosca round the tentadero. They repeated the same lessons for nearly an hour, José-Ramón finding faults where Francisco Javier was sure there were none, and when the señorito eventually called out that he'd done enough for that day he couldn't help enquiring with some impatience,

'But when am I going to learn something new?'

'You don't even know how to make a horse walk properly yet,' came the reply and then, crushingly, 'If all you want to do is cut a fine figure, don't expect me to waste time with you.'

He relented a little at Francisco Javier's hurt reaction.

'It's not my intention to teach you to show off on a horse. There are plenty of people who can do that already. Mosca is a horse of limited possibilities. So far you have nowhere reached his limits. When you do we'll start doing something else.'

Don Ramón's wife, Doña Sol, arrived one evening, accompanied by Mari-Angeles. She was too fashionably dressed for a country house and regally stiff. Domitila said that before the war she used to be much friendlier with everybody but now she was very formal and entirely given over to high society. Between them, mother and sister persuaded José-Ramón to return to Sevilla in time for the Rocío pilgrimage. They stayed overnight and the next morning Doña Sol left in the chauffeur-driven car.

Mari-Angeles rode back with her brother on a strawberry-grey horse borrowed from one of the herdsmen. Francisco Javier had the job of polishing him up and braiding his mane and tail. By the time they were ready to leave there was quite a different look about him and Mari-Angeles was very gratified, especially with his curls.

Francisco Javier went on practising with Mosca, ignoring Santiago who came to tease him. He practised behind the house, where Lolo and his sister did most of their riding. It seemed immense after the tentadero but he set his head confidently and worked Mosca on both reins as the señorito had taught him, crossing and recrossing the baked earth.

He was so accustomed now to slipping across Gavilán's back for a little while each night, promise forgotten, that

68

when the temptation to ride the chestnut colt in the tentadero presented itself he had no will-power to resist. He would ride him in the afternoon, just for a little while, when everyone was asleep, and make sure that saddle and bridle were back in their place long before Santiago had any chance of knowing they had even been used.

Remembering what had happened the last time Gavilán had seen his tack, he was very careful to have the tentadero gates shut before producing it. This time the colt didn't try to bolt but he was obviously distressed.

At the sight of the bridle he jerked his head higher and higher, backing across the arena and resisting all the boy's attempts to get his head down. Francisco Javier couldn't believe that Gavilán was just being contrary – his eyes looked too wild and frightened – so, remembering one of José-Ramón's bits of advice, 'Use your head before using any other part of your body', he put aside the bridle, talked and stroked the colt into a calmer frame, and then carefully saddled him.

Gavilán was still very jumpy but it was the bridle that seemed to upset him most, and Francisco Javier cinched up the girth without too much trouble. Then he unbuckled the reins and fitted them to the headcollar, thinking this a very clever solution.

Gavilán had quietened considerably but, in the saddle at last, Francisco Javier was very much aware of the extreme tension of the colt's muscles. His whole body seemed contracted, ready to spring, ready to shrink further, ready to explode. It was like sitting on a rumbling volcano and his instinct was to dismount before something untoward happened. Gavilán was infecting him with his own nervousness.

But that would be admitting defeat. Hadn't he calmed Gavilán so many times already, just by talking to him? So he didn't dismount. He just sat there and talked to him, as he did every night in the corral, and his own tension melted as he talked. Then he was silent, just feeling the horse, letting the minutes go by but unconscious of time.

'Come on, Gavilán. You know me. Stop messing about.' He said it in his head but he knew Gavilán heard him.

It was a strange sensation, feeling the colt unwind beneath him, and so much was he in tune with him that he even knew, just before it happened, when Gavilán was going to raise his flattened ears. He had been watching his ears and had almost willed him into relaxing them.

Eventually, and not before he knew he was ready for it, he asked him to walk and Gavilán responded with an ease that delighted him. They circled the tentadero twice on each rein with a smoothness beyond his imagination. It was quite different from those stolen rides in the corral. He knew that Gavilán was concentrating on his actions, that each stride was precise and perfectly judged, the last flowing into the next and giving a sensation of effortlessness.

He was very much tempted to ask more of him but, instinctively realizing that Gavilán had already done very much and would tense up again if pressed, he stopped. He leaned forward and hugged his arms round the colt's neck, burrowing his face in his mane, and Gavilán blew a long, relaxing snort and shook his head.

8

The return of the Casares family from Sevilla was accomplished with a great deal of bustle and excitement. The procession of horses and people was led by Don Ramón, who managed his carriage horses with great style and made no secret, anywhere along the way, of his pride in the four daughters and two grandsons who travelled with him. His sons and one son-in-law rode behind and Señor Juan and the stable lads brought up the rear with the rest of the horses, including two new ones.

They arrived in darkness, just before supper, and the patio was a mass of people and horses as everyone came out to greet the dusty travellers. People shouted, dogs barked, babies cried, horses whinnied and clattered. The sleepy fortress was suddenly alive again with laughter and exclamations.

Francisco Javier stood beside one of the arches, an unconscious smile on his face as he was enveloped by the warmth of this exuberant homecoming. For a little while he was part of the family. Don Ramón's smiles and open arms were wide enough to include everybody, right down to one of the dogs that impertinently jumped up at him, and it seemed only right and natural that Lolo should be showing off. He was making El Moro dance within his own length, front legs in the air, regardless of everyone pressed about, and with an expression of pretended consternation as if he was in no way responsible for the gelding's behaviour.

The grandchildren were passed from arms to eager arms to be hugged, kissed and crooned over, no one taking any notice of their screams; the four sisters each talked to several different people at one and the same time, and even José-Ramón for once looked as though he belonged among these noisy, excitable people.

Señor Juan was about very early the next morning, anxious to check on what had been happening while he was away. Gavilán had to be brought back to his stall but he wouldn't let Santiago catch him and Francisco Javier had to be sent to fetch him. Señor Juan berated both boys for giving Gavilán the freedom of the corral for so long. It would no doubt have gone to his head and then what would the señorito have to say? Santiago promptly put the blame on Francisco Javier and got a clout round the head from Señor Juan.

'You were in charge of him. Don't start on excuses with me!'

'It's true, it's true, and he's been riding him, too, and one day he let him escape and – '

He broke off with a yelp of fear as Señor Juan grabbed him by the ears and violently shook his head till he howled for mercy.

'You were in charge of him, you gutter-scum!' he roared.

From the corner of his eye he saw Francisco Javier backing away, trying to make himself scarce, and in a moment was on him, hard, horny fingers clamped round his neck.

'So, what's all this about then?' he asked in a dangerously soft voice that turned Francisco Javier's stomach to water.

'I didn't let him escape. He ran away but I caught him and he wasn't hurt. I promise,' he gabbled, hardly aware of what he was saying.

'But you rode him?' It was beyond Señor Juan's belief and

he was a very angry man. His fingernails pressed excruciatingly into Francisco Javier's neck.

'Yes, but . . . but the señorito knows about it and I haven't done it since.' The words came in desperate gasps.

He saw Santiago scramble to his feet and escape down one of the passages, holding his ears.

'Which señorito?'

'José-Ramón. He wasn't angry with me.'

'It's not his horse. If the other one hears of it I wouldn't like to be in your shoes. I told you to leave that colt alone. Why you boys can't just do as you're told . . . . Between you all, you'll be the death of me,' but his anger was waning, though he didn't relax his grip. 'What did the señorito say when he found out?'

'He said he'd teach me to ride, and he is teaching me.'

With a surprised oath, Señor Juan let him go. 'You'd better tell me all about it, boy, but if you're lying . . . .'

Francisco Javier hurriedly told him what had happened, almost truthfully, and Señor Juan was scratching his head by the time he'd finished.

'I don't like it,' he said after some silent thought. 'It'll cause trouble and when there's any trouble connected with the horses, I get it first, see. What the Señorito José-Ramón chooses to do is no business of mine, but just you keep away from Gavilán in future and don't get too big for your boots. You're still the last monkey around here.'

'Please let me look after Gavilán,' Francisco Javier begged him heedlessly. 'Santiago's scared of him but he and I, we get on perfectly. I can do anything with him.'

'And how well do you get on with the Señorito Manuel, or how long do you think you'd get on with him if he sees you can manage the colt better than he can?'

'I don't care.'

'No. I can see that, but you've got to learn some

73

discretion, boy. You're too proud. Leave that for the señoritos. They can afford it. If you get thrown out of this place, where will you go?'

The next afternoon Doña Sol arrived by car. It had been rumoured that she was bringing a famous torero with her, so everyone was hanging about, waiting to see him. Francisco Javier expected him to be dressed in his glittering costume. It was the only way he had ever seen a torero, on wall posters. He was very disappointed to see a small, thin man dressed in a cream-coloured suit and looking almost middle-aged, though he couldn't have been more than twenty-five. He was surrounded as he stepped out of the car, but his nonchalant attitude showed that he was used to receptions such as this and no doubt expected them.

Nearly all the boys who worked for Don Ramón wanted to be toreros and their excitement was great because surely he would be offered some heifers, which they might afterwards get a chance at, too. At the very least he would watch them practise cape movements and give them advice before going away, and if one of them drew his particular attention he might remember his name and mention it one day to his impresario. There was always that hope, and Francisco Javier recognized in their eyes and faces the same passion he had seen in Pepe's. It was a fever that left its own mark.

But none of this affected him very deeply, beyond an ache in his breast as he thought of Pepe and wished he could be among these boys. His mind was mostly occupied with becoming Gavilán's groom, in spite of Señor Juan's emphatic refusal. He'd even thought of asking Lolo himself but was scared of Señor Juan's reaction should the señorito capriciously agree.

He had already learned that there were ways of doing everything and that the wrong way could be disastrous. He knew that asking José-Ramón would jeopardize his chances altogether – perhaps the riding lessons, too – and yet he couldn't give up. Santiago was equally anxious to be rid of Gavilán but, just now, his head was taken up with the torero and nothing else mattered.

Could he ask Mari-Angeles? She had brought him a present, the first he had ever received in his life. It was for turning out the strawberry horse so well. She gave it to him when the whole family came down to ride the afternoon after their arrival, so everyone watched while he unwrapped and opened the box at her insistence. It was a brown, Cordoba hat.

He refused to try it on just then, sure that everyone would laugh at him, especially Lolo who exclaimed with a grin, 'So now we have a pig with a hat, eh!' As soon as he was free of them, however, he raced to the kitchen to look at himself in Domitila's mirror, and he liked what he saw.

Domitila rubbed some dirt off his cheek and set the hat at the right angle, but he spent quite some time tipping it first one way and then another, practising different expressions and grinning at himself. He told himself he would only wear it for special occasions, and for his lessons.

Yes, the señorita might be a possibility.

Señor Juan gave him one of the new horses to look after, a pure white, grey-muzzled Andalusian stallion called Nevado which had been bought by José-Ramón. Nevado was stronger-looking and taller than Gavilán, a beautiful creature with large eyes and straight head, perfectly rounded body and magnificent mane and tail. It didn't take him long to make friends with Nevado and, had he not been so obsessed with Gavilán, he would have been proud to have him in his care. Now, however, he felt his chances with Gavilán were even more remote.

Even though José-Ramón was back the riding lessons didn't start again. The usual routine was completely disordered by the presence of so many people and Señor Juan was suddenly an unbearable task-master, venting his annoyance on all and sundry. Horses were ordered and then not required, or required without any anticipation, and half the time the stable boys were dreaming of bulls instead of concentrating on the work in hand. Family and friends made long, evening excursions on horseback, spent most of the night talking in the patio, and rarely showed any signs of life before eleven or twelve o'clock the next morning.

This was the hour all the boys eagerly awaited, when the torero exercised his art on the heifers brought up from the pastures. He needed assistants and had a dozen amateurs to call on from ten years old upwards. There wasn't a boy to be found in the patio after twelve o'clock. They were all in the tentadero.

One morning everyone begged Don Ramón to give them a display of rejoneo, but he was not to be drawn. He was out of practice, he said, and Jubiloso was better at chasing bulls than being confronted by them.

Lolo offered himself instead and Francisco Javier watched with great anticipation. He knew nothing of rejoneo, except that the rider used his horse to tempt his foe instead of a cape, and was eager to learn what Gaviota had been so famous for in years gone by. However, neither El Moro nor Manzanares reacted very well when attacked by a two-year-old heifer of unquenchable bravery. They seemed stiff and unyielding and Lolo used his spurs a great deal. Someone commented that if he managed to get close to the heifer it was because the horses were more afraid of Lolo than the horns. Francisco Javier, expecting much, was very disappointed.

Several days went by before he saw José-Ramón alone when, for once, he came down at his usual early hour in spite of having gone to bed only a few hours before. He asked for Nevado to be saddled and, while waiting, said, 'What do you think of him?'

'He's really beautiful, señorito. Is he better than Lucero?'

'He's different, not better, and he's been well-trained. I thought I would never convince his owner to part with him. When we know each other we should get on very well. When are you going to wear your hat?' he then smiled at him. 'No one's seen you in it yet.'

'When you give me the next lesson,' Francisco Javier replied, unable to disguise either his hope or misgiving.

'A glutton for punishment, eh?' the señorito returned with a grin. 'The fact is, I'm leaving here soon. My father has some land that belonged to my uncle. What with the war and the drought and other problems nothing much has been done there in years. I'm going to take it over – breed my own horses, among other things – and I'd like you to come with me, to look after Lucero and Nevado. We can go on with the lessons then, and you can wear your hat.'

He obviously expected an enthusiastic response, and the smile in his eyes faded when met by Francisco Javier's crestfallen silence.

'Well, what do you say?' he asked with surprised impatience.

'It's just that . . . .'

Francisco Javier didn't know how to reply, torn between opposing desires, knowing that whatever he said he couldn't have both the things he wanted above all else – to work for the señorito and yet keep Gavilán – and still too numb to think.

'Do you want to come or don't you? Just say.'

'What about Gaviota? I have to look after her. She's very fond of me.'

Any excuse for avoiding a decision right now.

'Someone else can be found or perhaps we can take her with us. She lived there for years, after all. I'll see what my father says. So?' The searching look required an answer.

He dropped his eyes and mumbled, 'It's Gavilán. I don't want to leave him. More than anything else I want to be with him.'

There was a short, cold silence. José-Ramón hadn't expected, and didn't like, the refusal. He turned to mount Nevado and with a bareness of expression said, 'As you wish,' and rode away.

9

In the days that followed Francisco Javier felt the bleakness of his brief, early morning encounters with José-Ramón. Now he realized just how much he had come to depend on the señorito's reserved but genuine benevolence. Without it he felt as lost as when he had first been brought here. He was a nobody again – the last monkey, as Señor Juan was often reminding him.

He felt even worse when Mari-Angeles unexpectedly attacked him with blazing eyes and scornful words.

'What an ungrateful churl you are. I don't know why I ever troubled myself over you. I would never have brought you the hat if I'd known how you'd repay us,' she exclaimed, flouncing off with satisfaction as tears smarted in his eyes.

It was only then he realized that the señorito was more than offended, although in his bewildered misery he couldn't understand any further than this. Surely José-Ramón couldn't believe he was seeking Lolo's favour in preference to his own? And even if he did think this why should it trouble him so much, and Mari-Angeles too?

He felt more and more miserable as José-Ramón continued unbendingly aloof and would have given anything to be able to take back his reply, or at least to have the chance to phrase it differently, explain his reason. But in his present mood, which made Francisco Javier feel cold to his toes, José-Ramón was unapproachable.

He sought consolation with the horses, because they were

the only ones who would accept either his words or his silence without questioning his loyalty, and his anguish was increased when he saw how much Gavilán needed him.

The chestnut colt had very much regressed since being back in the patio, and Santiago made no pretence of bearing with him. He complained loudly at being obliged to look after him and, whenever Señor Juan wasn't around, meanly repaid all the bites and frights he got.

As often as he could Francisco Javier talked to the colt and stroked him, but it was as if all those hours spent together in the corral now meant nothing. Gavilán showed the whites of his eyes and jerked back his head, as if expecting a blow from the raised hand rather than a caress, and the only time he seemed at peace was when he was alone.

How could he possibly abandon Gavilán, seeing him like this? If he could regain the señorito's favour only at the colt's expense, he knew he would have to do without it, and he grew angry himself because José-Ramón should have seen and understood.

Señor Juan put another boy to look after Gavilán but it made no difference. The chestnut colt seemed to hate everybody. Lolo rode him every evening on the family excursions but even before they set out from the patio Gavilán was tossing his head about, rolling his eyes, sweating up, regardless of the rest of the horses standing quietly by.

'That horse is crazy,' the torero exclaimed to Lolo who laughingly shrugged off his remark.

He liked a challenge and was determined to get the better of Gavilán sooner or later. He rode him with both curb and serreta, to which the principal reins were attached. This at least kept his head controlled without punishing his mouth, but his nose was rubbed raw because he fought and fretted all the way.

Eventually Francisco Javier realized that Gavilán was

afraid, and that his fear began just as soon as he was saddled and bridled for Lolo to ride. He was terrified of Lolo, not because of any punishment he might receive – although this secondary fear was also growing – but because he was utterly confused by him.

Señor Juan knew it was because of Lolo, too, although he wouldn't say this in so many words. Only he or Don Ramón could do something about it, but Don Ramón had sufficient confidence in his son's judgement to leave him to get on with Gavilán in his own way, and Señor Juan was in no hurry to be at loggerheads with the señorito.

Only Francisco Javier was prepared to stick his neck out and, in the end, Señor Juan said he could look after Gavilán, hoping that somehow the boy might improve the situation or bring it to the boil. He felt no compunction about using him in this way. He'd already warned him enough.

Lolo didn't object. He was aware that the boy had turned down his brother's request and thought it would be one in the eye for him. But there was no sense of triumph in Francisco Javier's heart.

'I see you've got what you wanted,' José-Ramón said to him with icy expression, not seeming to understand that he wasn't happy and that he hadn't planned it like this.

As Señor Juan had foretold, Lolo was soon irritated by Francisco Javier's obvious empathy with Gavilán. He managed to present a calm, compliant horse that didn't start acting up until his rider appeared on the scene.

'That horse doesn't like you, Lolo,' his brother-in-law remarked with a laugh one evening, which certainly did nothing to improve his temper.

When Francisco Javier scraped the dust and sweat off the colt that night his fingers found blood on both flanks. It was too dark then to verify the cause of it, although he knew without needing to look. Rage hammered in his heart. Lolo was in the patio, sharing jokes and a bottle of wine with his

81

brother-in-law and the torero, and strong words of accusation choked in Francisco Javier's throat. He wished Gavilán would throw Lolo one day and break his neck.

When the torero's short holiday was over the daily sessions in the tentadero ended, too, although the most determined of the amateurs continued to practise with their capes, real or improvised, in the evening shadows. They gathered on the river bank, swam and larked about, and took it in turns to play bull to each other. Francisco Javier joined them sometimes, but only as spectator and critic. He discovered that his opinion had a certain value among them and was quick to enlarge on his adventures with Pepe, to whom he gave heroic proportions. They didn't always believe him but were glad enough to listen.

With nothing else to do in the mornings, Lolo re-embarked on Gavilán's schooling. At first Francisco Javier watched, Gaviota nodding off beside him. He hadn't seen Lolo at work with a horse since José-Ramón had started to give him lessons – which now seemed in another time – and he remembered how he had been struck with admiration. But now he was less ignorant.

José-Ramón had on one occasion demonstrated with Lucero the truly established communion of horse and rider, where effort had been eliminated by the sheer perfection of the simplest movement. He had displayed no extravagant airs, just the walk, trot and canter both extended and collected, but with such artistry that Francisco Javier had needed no one to tell him that it couldn't be done better than this. Remy had been right.

After only a little while he couldn't bear to watch Lolo any longer. Even making allowances for a difficult horse – which was his fault anyway – the complete lack of understanding between them jarred too heavily. Lolo's language was force and, although he controlled it admirably and to a fine degree, it could never translate into harmony. With a horse of Gavilán's calibre it was entirely self-defeating.

Again and again Lolo returned Gavilán to the patio with the marks of his spurs on him and in so jaded a condition that Francisco Javier was hard put to keep his feelings to himself. In just a few days there was a gauntness about the colt that no amount of good feeding could repair.

'It's his nerves,' said Señor Juan, looking at him with disgust. 'They eat up every ounce of food we put in him.'

'Can't anything be done?' Francisco Javier begged him, knowing exactly what this man thought of the situation and unable to understand why he did nothing. 'Don Ramón should be told.'

'You just keep your mouth shut. Something will happen one of these days without your provoking it and, if you know what's good for you, when that time comes you'll keep well out of it.' Recognizing Francisco Javier's contempt for this advice, he added, 'Heed what I say, boy. I know what I'm talking about.'

Something did happen, only a couple of days later.

It was on the morning that Don Ramón's bull-breeding friend, Don Felix, came to pay a visit. Don Felix had recently sold a young seed bull to Don Ramón which was now in a corral behind the tentadero, to be released just as soon as Don Ramón had assured himself that the animal had come to no harm on the journey and was in perfect health. Don Felix had driven over to check up on his bull, using this as an excuse for bringing along his daughter, and his wife.

In Domitila's kitchen that morning there was both speculation and criticism of Don Felix's daughter, Conchita. Everyone agreed she was very beautiful, although Francisco Javier personally preferred Mari-Angeles. According to Domitila she and José-Ramón had loved each other since childhood and their engagement had been announced during his summer leave before the battle of the Ebro. Since then they had been very cool with each other and it was said that Conchita had other admirers. No one could blame her, under the circumstances, but she was engaged, after all, and the engagement had never been officially renounced.

The several women there each had their own opinion of the situation, some blaming José-Ramón rather than Conchita, and after a while Francisco Javier left them to it, thoroughly bored. He went back to Gaviota who hadn't wanted to leave her stall that day. It was one of her bad days, when she was lame and feeling her years, and he had originally gone to the kitchen for a few apples or carrots to cheer her up.

At mid-day all the men were in the patio, sampling Don Ramón's best manzanilla and smoking his cigars. Señor Juan had been invited to join them, and they sat in a semi-circle of stiff-backed chairs talking bulls and horses. Lolo wasn't among them. He was out with Gavilán and Francisco Javier was waiting for him to return, sitting on the manger at Gaviota's head.

Suddenly Lolo appeared in the patio, on foot and without Gavilán. There was blood spattered over his shirt and smeared on his face. Don Ramón sprang up with an oath of concern but Lolo nonchalantly waved him back.

'It's all right. It's only my nose. Don't get alarmed.'

He doused his face in the water trough and then took the chair Señor Juan had risen to offer him.

'That damned horse needs shooting,' he said. 'He's bats, demented, a maniac – '

'But what happened?' demanded Don Ramón with raised voice.

'What happened? He suddenly went mad, that's what happened. Bucking and rearing and whirling round like a rabid dog. In the end he threw me and galloped off. I landed on my face, that's all.'

'You've split your lip,' said Don Felix with amusement, offering him a handkerchief. 'Pour him a glass of wine, Ramón. That's all the doctoring he needs.'

Lolo leaned his chair backwards and yelled out to Francisco Javier, knowing he was somewhere behind him, 'Paco, go and look for the horse.'

'Do you know where he is, señorito?' asked Señor Juan as Francisco Javier approached.

Lolo shrugged and, ignoring him, said to Francisco Javier, 'He ran off through the trees behind the house. Start looking there. With a bit of luck he might have broken his neck. If he hasn't, when you bring him back I'll ride him again.'

'You won't ride him again,' José-Ramón put in very quietly, the suppressed rage with which he spoke drawing everyone's attention. Francisco Javier felt a sudden leap of hope, almost disbelief.

'You just keep out of this. It's none of your business,' Lolo snapped at him, eyes hard with antagonism. 'You, Paco, go and look for the horse.'

But Francisco Javier hardly heard him, lost in astonishment at José-Ramón's unexpected interference. He hung about as Don Ramón tried to reason with his elder son.

'Lolo's right. You can't let a horse get away with something like that. He's got to ride him again.'

'Papa, you don't know anything about it. Lolo's made a mess of that horse from the very beginning and he's been misusing him for weeks. You could have seen it for yourself if you weren't of the opinion that everything he does is beyond reproach.'

'Be careful with what you say,' shouted Don Ramón, instantly inflamed, but José-Ramón wasn't impressed by his father's anger.

'Gavilán could have been another Gaviota but for this

brother of mine who'd do better as a mule-driver than anything else. He doesn't know a good horse from a pile of bricks.'

All three were on their feet now, in open conflict, regardless of their guests and anyone else.

'It's easy for you to talk,' sneered Lolo. 'What do you know about that horse? I'd like to see what you could do with him.'

'At this moment, nothing, probably, but – '

'But what? You can say what you like, knowing no one's going to expect you to prove it. You ride him when that boy gets him back. Show us all how clever you are.'

There was an electric silence as everyone automatically looked at José-Ramón to see if the challenge would be taken up. He couldn't get out of it without losing the right to interfere in Lolo's plans or without losing face, but even before he spoke Francisco Javier was certain he would reject it, for Gavilán's sake. His heart burned at Lolo's unfairness.

'That's just the kind of reaction one would expect from you,' was the scornful reply.

'And you're going to wriggle out of it with words. I know you, brother. Until you can prove yourself the superior, you'd do better to mind your own business.'

'Come, come,' broke in Don Ramón in an effort to restore harmony. 'What's Don Felix going to think? Forget the horse. It's not important. We'll talk about it another day.'

José-Ramón lost all restraint at these words, turning on his father a look of anguish. 'Stop protecting me,' he cried. 'I don't need it. All I need is for you to have faith in me, to stop looking on me as a war cripple.'

Don Ramón was taken aback, left speechless for a moment. 'I don't do that,' he then passionately protested.

'Don't you? Perhaps you don't notice after three years. You let Lolo have Gavilán and Princesa in the first place

86

because you didn't think I'd have much use for horses. And right this minute you share his belief that, as a cripple, I couldn't manage a difficult horse, and you don't want me to embarrass you in front of Don Felix.'

'Hush lad. Your father doesn't think that,' interrupted Don Felix, hoping to reduce his agitation.

José-Ramón ignored him. 'Papa, are you going to listen to me or not? Are you going to stop him riding Gavilán again?'

'You know I don't like to interfere between the two of you,' blustered Don Ramón with an expression of pained bewilderment, though still very much provoked by his son's accusation, so bitterly shouted at him. 'It has nothing to do with me. If it bothered you so much about Lolo having Gavilán and Princesa you should have said so at the time.'

'You haven't answered me,' José-Ramón insisted, looking very much like his brother just then, very proud, as with obvious irony he went on to contradict himself. 'Well, yes, you have answered. You don't believe in me.'

Don Ramón expressed his exasperation with a string of swear-words which his son tersely cut short.

'Then I accept my brother's challenge. I'll show you all how clever I am but in my way, not his. Do you agree to that, Father?'

His sudden calm, and his hard pronunciation of the last word, made Francisco Javier's heart clench. There was something ominous in it.

Don Ramón was always suspicious of his son's cold logic. He was sure there was a trick in this, somewhere. 'What do you mean?' he said cautiously.

'All I ask is permission to prove myself the superior, as my brother suggests; to demonstrate to you, and anyone else' – his contemptuous glance fell on everybody, including Francisco Javier – 'that I'm as much a man with one arm as I was with two.'

'What do you want to do?' replied Don Ramón, evading

87

the issue, frightened by the look in his son's eyes.

'What does it matter?'

Don Ramón looked as though he would burst at such provocation. 'All right, all right,' he exclaimed at last. 'Whatever you say.'

'No recantation,' insisted his son. 'Don Felix is a witness.'

'To the devil with it,' roared Don Ramón. 'Do what you like.'

'A short while ago my brother gave a lamentable display of rejoneo. Well, this evening I'll give a better one and to you, Papa, I'll dedicate the three rosettes I intend to nail home – one for each horse you're going to give me if I succeed.'

Lolo scoffed but Don Ramón's first irritated reaction was to say, 'The heifers have all gone back to the pastures. It'll have to be another day.'

José-Ramón shook his head with a grim smile. 'Don Felix's bull,' he said.

A torrent of abuse burst from Don Ramón while his friend sat back and laughed heartily.

'You're crazy. You've tricked me and I'll not hear of it. No, no and no. You think I'll let you risk your life for such stupidity?'

'It'll be Lucero's life, not mine. You'll have less to lose than I will.'

'The bull could get you, too, and you know it.'

José-Ramón shrugged indifferently.

'He's only suggested it because he knows you won't let him do it,' put in Lolo.

'Shut up,' snapped Don Ramón.

He sat down on his chair again and motioned for José-Ramón to do the same. Then he pulled out a handkerchief to wipe the sweat from his face.

'You don't know what you're saying,' he said defeatedly. 'And all for a horse.'

'It's for myself, not for a horse.'

'You don't have to prove anything to me, son. Didn't my own sister teach you horsemanship and wasn't she the best horsewoman of the century?' He was pleading now. 'You can have Princesa, and Gavilán if you want him, and any other horse – '

José-Ramón interrupted him impatiently. 'I'll choose the horses I want when I've earned them – one rosette, one horse.'

'But why rosettes? Make do with the spears . . . .'

Don Felix made a complaining noise. 'That bull's already taken the steel too many times,' he saw fit to remind his friend. 'Surely you're not going to open him up again?'

'My son is more important than your bull. My bull,' he corrected himself.

'Then let him do what he wants and we can all drink this good wine of yours without having it turn sour in our stomachs.'

'But what can I say to your mother?' groaned Don Ramón helplessly. 'If she were in Sevilla . . . . But she's here and she'll blame me.'

'Tell her not to worry, that I can do it easily,' was the haughty reply.

Don Ramón suddenly turned on his younger son. 'All this is your doing,' he shouted at him. 'If you weren't such an idiot!'

Lolo jumped up with a scarcely withheld oath on his lips. 'Go and find that horse,' he shouted at Francisco Javier and marched off to the house, fuming.

10

Gavilán was by the river again. His chest on the offside was scraped and dusty, his body still patchily dark with sweat. It looked as though he must have tripped over the reins which dragged on the ground, one set broken, but at least he was sound in all four limbs, as he quickly demonstrated by trotting off with flattened ears at Francisco Javier's approach.

'Come on now,' he coaxed. 'You know I'm not Lolo. And no one's going to hurt you any more. You'll see.'

Gavilán listened to him but wouldn't let him get near. He tossed his head and rolled his eyes and nervously circled about, ready to race off again. For once he wasn't interested in the grass.

'All right,' called Francisco Javier with a shrug, halting. 'You've got all day. So have I.'

He pulled off his clothes and splashed about in the river for a while, knowing it would take time to deceive Gavilán in his present state and that any rushing now would make things worse. The barley he had put in his pockets he spread out on his shirt, hoping it might tempt the colt but not expecting quick reactions, and when the sun burned too hotly on him, even though he was in the water, he looked for some shade and sat down to wait.

It was difficult to be patient. Although there was delight in his heart at Lolo's downfall, and even now he couldn't help grinning at the memory of his bloody face, he was in a state of turmoil for José-Ramón, and knew enough of bulls to be terribly afraid for Lucero.

Lonely himself, having no one to love or love him and sensitive, therefore, to the smallest kindnesses, he couldn't help identifying with José-Ramón who was the only person to have regarded him with any real interest ever since he had lost Pepe. And his own heart ached with hurt pride, burned with indignation, lurched with fear, as his mind played over the morning's events and anticipated the evening's.

All of a sudden he felt Gavilán's breath on his neck as the colt blew through his nostrils behind him. Very gently he reached for the reins, and stood up without startling him. He ran his fingers softly along the colt's neck while looking for the hurts he might have sustained, and wasn't surprised to see the freshly bleeding scores on his flanks or the broken swelling on his nose.

But he suddenly went cold inside when he noticed the blood stains round his jaws. Gavilán backed away from him with an agitated whicker when he tried to examine his mouth, but he saw enough to know that Lolo must have lost his temper or deliberately used the curb to punish him. No wonder Gavilán had gone beserk.

'It's a pity you only ran away,' he said, hugging his neck. 'You should have kicked his head in while you had the chance.'

When they returned there was no one in the patio but Señor Juan, who this time allowed himself to say out loud what he thought of the Señorito Manuel.

'When you've cleaned that horse up take him over to one of the corrals and turn him loose. Don Ramón says he's not to be ridden any more.'

'What will he do with him? He won't shoot him, will he? It wasn't Gavilán's fault. You know that. Look at his mouth.'

'Just turn him loose and stop worrying. You'd do better to worry about Lucero. It's the craziest thing I've ever heard and if we haven't got a horse with a hole through his breast

91

by nightfall I might even start going to mass again.'

'Is what the señorito's going to do really dangerous?'

'The only way to plant those rosettes is over the horns, which means the horse and the bull have got to throw themselves at each other like two steam-engines on the same track. At the last moment Lucero's got to swerve just enough to miss the horn but stay close enough for the señorito to lean right out of the saddle to plant the rosette.'

'But how can he do it without reins?' cried Francisco Javier, aghast.

'It's not impossible. I've seen it done. It was one of Señorita Angeles' favourite tricks with Gaviota. But there's no room for mistakes.'

'Do you think he can do it, Señor Juan?' he begged, eyes wide with fear.

'He thinks he can or he wouldn't have suggested it. He cares a great deal for Lucero.'

Francisco Javier made a special effort with Gavilán's appearance before turning him away. He washed him all over to remove every trace of blood and sweat and dust, walked him round and round the patio in the sun till he dried, combed out his mane, forelock and tail as if preparing him for a special occasion, oiled his hooves, and worked till his arms ached to bring out the sunglow of his skin.

It was good for both of them. Gavilán was gentle again and Francisco Javier had adjusted to José-Ramón's intentions. Faith in him had flowered. Even though he had seen him do nothing spectacular on horseback – unlike Lolo and Mari-Angeles and even Don Ramón – he had witnessed that short display of basic horsemanship and was sure that Lucero would respond unfalteringly to whatever was asked of him.

Most of the boys were sitting on the wall overlooking the penned bull and he joined them to listen to their comments and make his own. The bull had the unfortunate name of Matajaca – horse-killer – because as a two-year-old he had fatally overturned a horse at his bravery test. He stared curiously up at the boys who attracted his attention, before returning to the pile of grass that had been cut for him, and there was both innocence and nobility in his expression.

He represented four hundred and sixty-three kilos of bone and muscle, coated in glistening ebony, and the scars of his courage were still there to see on the hump at the base of his neck. His horns were perfectly shaped, with a slight upward tilt to their needle-point tips. Just now he was as quiet as any of the steers bunched on the other side of his pen, but it was the calm of the killer who knows his own strength and has no need to flaunt it.

'Don Felix says he charges straight and true,' one of the boys remarked.

'Don Ramón's given orders for his horns to be capped.'

There was a groan of disappointment at this. With only half the danger there would be only half the excitement, and Francisco Javier felt ashamed of himself for being relieved, even as he echoed their sentiments.

'Does the señorito know?' someone else asked, but nobody could say.

This gave rise to speculation on what would happen when he found out, if he didn't know, and there was much delighted anticipation of another row between father and son. Francisco Javier slipped away, not wanting to listen. He went back to Gaviota, who showed her pleasure at the sight of him by rubbing her head so hard against his chest that she hurt him.

'Ay, Gaviota,' he sighed. 'I hope Lucero is as clever and as brave as you.'

It was too hot to sleep on his mattress so he stayed with Gaviota, lying down under the manger so that she couldn't accidentally tread on him. He didn't want to think or worry any more so he shut his eyes and listened to all the movements and sounds of horses and people, struck by the sweetness of the song that suddenly burst from one of the canaries and tirelessly rose and fell. Like this, he fell asleep.

Señor Juan roused him a couple of hours later to tell him that José-Ramón wanted both Lucero and Nevado saddled. He set to work with alacrity, needing action to calm his nerves. The other boys crowded round while he worked, commenting on Lucero as if they had never seen him before, wanting to squeeze every last ounce of flavour from the event. They showed almost religious deference as they made way for José-Ramón when he came to check Lucero's tack, and listened uninvited while he gave instructions to Antonio and Fermín, who had been chosen to run the bull for him.

Francisco Javier didn't envy either of them, except on Pepe's behalf. What wouldn't he have done for a chance like this! It was undoubtedly a signal honour but they both looked green with dread. It was one thing to make a few passes at a two-year-old heifer and quite another to incite a four hundred and sixty-three kilo bull, even with padded horns, but still they wanted to do it.

After dragging for so long, the time suddenly flew. José-Ramón and Señor Juan went off with the horses, the boys made for the tentadero to watch Matajaca have his horns padded, the patio emptied of people and noise. Francisco Javier went to put on his hat. If this wasn't a special occasion then there never would be one in all his life.

The tentadero was occupied on both sunny and shady sides, everybody from the house being there as well as quite a few herdsmen and labourers. Don Ramón was trying to look confident without altogether successfully hiding his anxiety and Lolo, beside him, was his usual, arrogant self in spite of his bruised, swollen face. Nothing upset him for long. Perhaps he still expected a laugh at his brother's expense.

It was difficult for anyone to guess what Doña Sol was feeling. She sat straight and still between Don Felix's wife and daughter and only her fan, which moved with more agitation than grace, gave any hint of her thoughts. Conchita, beside Mari-Angeles, was even stiller. The eyes of both were fixed on José-Ramón who, mounted on Nevado, was carrying on some kind of argument with the men responsible for the bull. He seemed in no hurry to start the performance and next had a conversation with Señor Juan who showed him the rosettes, whose blue and red colours Don Ramón's bulls had carried into rings all over the country before the war.

There were many shouts and hisses for silence as eventually the arena emptied of all but the milk-white stallion and his rider, dressed in grey. José-Ramón raised his hat to his family before taking up the reins and soon the only thing to be heard was the soft, neat fall of Nevado's hooves as he tracked to the left at a collected trot, one ear forward, one back, eager but perfectly controlled.

There was no other sound as José-Ramón guided him through a series of half-passes to right and left, coaxed him into elevated trots on the spot and from thence into a floating trot in turns and circles of incredible smoothness. The look of concentration on the rider's face was matched by the sharp alertness of the horse's ears.

Nevado was absolutely confident and at ease, even though every muscle of his body was in play, and the flying changes, the pirouettes performed at incredible speed and yet without a single false movement, were but the physical expression of an intimate dialogue between man and beast in perfect harmony.

It was over far too soon for Francisco Javier, who was jerked out of his dream-like enchantment when he saw

Señor Juan appear in the open gateway with Lucero. Amid applause and shouts of appreciation, José-Ramón walked Nevado over to them, dismounted, checked Lucero's girth and mounted again.

Now the excitement was getting out of hand. Much as José-Ramón's skill as a horseman might be appreciated, they were there to watch him risk Lucero's life and perhaps his own. Doña Sol and Conchita had still hardly moved.

The gates were closed again. José-Ramón cantered a couple of circles to warm Lucero up, made him cross the tentadero once on each rein at a showy half-pass, reined him back ten paces in a straight line and halted him squarely in front of the bull-gate on the opposite side of the ring. Meanwhile, Señor Juan edged up beside Francisco Javier at the barrier, the rosettes in his hand. He pushed them onto the boy.

'The señorito wants you to look after these, so you'd better stick close and be on your toes.'

Francisco Javier was speechless. Such a gesture must mean he'd been forgiven, was perhaps even a peace offering. Choked with pride, and the momentary centre of attention, he took the handful of barbed silks and hurried round to where José-Ramón had stationed himself.

The men were up on the bull-gates, waiting for José-Ramón's signal which came with a nod of his head. Antonio, the first assistant, slipped from behind his burladero and waited for the bull to appear, holding a pink and yellow cape that had been loaned to him for the occasion.

Matajaca entered the tentadero at a swift trot, head raised, ears well forward, his proud, confident bearing drawing exclamations of approval that swelled into shouts of surprise and a wild buzz of comment as everyone saw his long, bared horns.

'So that's why he was playing about beforehand,' a

96

herdsman behind Francisco Javier exclaimed, obviously impatient of the display with Nevado.

'He's more astute than his father is, that one,' someone replied in admiring tones, proceeding to clamour his satisfaction, as everyone else was doing.

Don Ramón was on his feet, shouting and gesticulating furiously, but was withheld from any further action by the combined efforts of his family and Don Felix. At last he sat down again, still protesting, and he missed young Antonio's great moment as he spurred Matajaca into his first rush of the evening with the flaring of the cape round his body.

Don Ramón hadn't chosen Don Felix's seed bull only for his beauty. In half a second he had exploded into a rushing mass of fury, going for the lure with the speed of a race-horse, losing it and turning in his tracks without any waste of movement. At the second pass his right horn ripped the cape from Antonio's fingers and, while he tossed it over his shoulders, Antonio dived for the burladero to the sound of slightly mocking cheers.

Fermin cited Matajaca from the opposite side. He was being very brave, calling him almost from the centre of the arena, and Matajaca bore down on him like a mountain landslide, distracted at the last moment by the cape that swept him past the boy's breast with only an inch to spare. This, and his next three passes, drew a chorus of 'olés' from the spectators.

Meanwhile, José-Ramón sat quietly on Lucero, watching the bull's every movement. On this short assessment Lucero's life would depend. Matajaca obviously favoured his right horn, responded instantly, and turned without losing much ground. Lucero watched the bull with the same concentration as his rider, his dark ears seeming to stretch, his eyes dilating.

Fermin very neatly left Matajaca facing man and horse, then slipped away. The bull looked from side to side imperiously, wondering where the capes had got to, believing perhaps that he'd already vanquished them. He was arrogantly beautiful, standing squarely there, afraid of nothing, killer instinct roused. He looked at José-Ramón and Lucero but, used to herdsmen, wasn't altogether interested in them.

José-Ramón, pressing Lucero into a slow dance, called out in a challenging tone, 'Hey, bull!' It was all the provocation Matajaca needed.

He threw himself at this new enemy and Lucero moved to meet him, cutting across the bull's track at such a collected gallop that surely José-Ramón's judgement must be wrong. Francisco Javier could see the horns nail right through Lucero's gleaming haunch. But, at the last moment, the gelding sprang ahead and Matajaca swept past his tail.

Man and horse turned to face him again. Matajaca had turned almost as rapidly and the two galloping animals were bound to collide, horn against shoulder, except that after breathless seconds Lucero pulled ahead, again only by inches. Matajaca kept up the chase and the spectators howled with excitement as José-Ramón kept Lucero only just ahead of the bull, slowing him whenever Matajaca lost ground, giving him his head just as the horns were about to hook his hocks, smoothly in control in spite of Lucero's very real fear.

The bull tired of this and turned to look for the previous lures, trotting with pricked ears towards the burladero where he remembered one of them had disappeared. He could see someone's head and began battering at the woodwork with his horns. Lucero came up behind him, stopping at hardly four lengths' distance to perform an on-the-spot dance as insolent as it was flawless, and pirouetting away from Matajaca's thunderbolt charge as if it was the easiest thing in the world. How the onlookers yelled!

Again the two animals raced, one pursuing, one pursued.

This time Matajaca was determined to succeed, perhaps remembering that horse he had overturned in the pastures. There were sounds of anguish from the spectators as José-Ramón made no effort to disengage him, leading him through a series of turns that had a savage grace. With complete disregard for danger, he rode Lucero right up to the boards where, trapped between Matajaca and the barrier, there was no escape for them except in speed.

Lucero's terror couldn't be doubted. It was in his eyes, his widely flared nostrils, his flattened ears. But he responded instantly when José-Ramón forced him in one great leap straight across the bull's path to freedom. By the time Matajaca had pulled himself up Lucero was over on the other side, well out of his way.

It seemed to Francisco Javier as though half a lifetime had passed instead of a few minutes. His clothes were stuck to him and his heart beat so fast that he felt quite dizzy. He could only really believe that both horse and rider were out of danger when he saw José-Ramón calmly knotting the reins as he usually did before a riding lesson, and almost expected him to pull out his cigarettes. Instead he stretched out his hand for the first rosette.

Matajaca was still looking for trouble. The very sight of Lucero on the move again made him spurt into action, putting his opponents at a disadvantage. José-Ramón had only a few minutes to plant the three rosettes before Lucero began to slow through sheer exhaustion, yet the seconds flew by as Matajaca kept too close to be suitably manoeuvred. The chance came as Lucero swirled to the left and Matajaca had to follow his charge through to the right and both turned to seek each other again, on the same track in opposing directions.

Francisco Javier involuntarily shut his eyes at the imminent head-on collision, opening them again at the almost hysterical shouts behind him as the bull came away

99

from the encounter with the first red and blue ribbon fluttering on his neck. He shook his high held head angrily, as if bothered by a hornet.

José-Ramón galloped Lucero back to the barrier, calling for the second rosette. Francisco Javier ran out with it, feeling it snatched from his fingers as Lucero swirled past him and went straight into the attack a second time because Matajaca was standing absolutely squarely in the centre of the arena, a perfect target.

The bull was off the mark just as quickly and this time Francisco Javier kept his eyes open – he hardly had time to shut them. The line of attack was so straight that he couldn't even seen the bull until Lucero's last-moment swerve brought Matajaca galloping towards him with the second rosette nailed beside the first. The great shoulders were within touching distance as Matajaca paused by the barrier, heaving with exertion. His wet muzzle gleamed in the sunlight. Francisco Javier almost loved him just then for his honest rage and his spirit.

He had to run round to the other side of the tentadero with the third rosette as Matajaca showed no inclination to move away unless provoked, needing a breathing space too.

The third charge was as clean as the second but Lucero lost his nerve and deliberately skipped out of it just as José-Ramón leaned to meet the bull, almost leaving his rider on the horns. Doña Sol's scream was louder than anyone else's. The rosette dropped to the sand, but José-Ramón miraculously regained his balance and spurred Lucero angrily towards the barrier for another one. He looked shaken and strained.

There was a stubborn expression in Lucero's white-rimmed eyes which faded as José-Ramón sat him quietly for a few moments and stroked his neck. They had approached the barrier at odds with each other, Lucero smarting with punishment, his rider with anger, but in those few seconds they made their peace with each other and were ready to try again.

José-Ramón took Lucero calmly away from the bull, intending to turn him into another frontal attack, but Matajaca was already after them again and they had to race away from him. They lost him in a figure of eight movement that, perfectly judged, brought Lucero bouncing back towards his enemy, snorting with excitement, ears pricked, eyes bulging. But this time he trusted his rider and the horns directed at his breast just swept past his shoulder.

There were rapturous shouts and hand clapping as the third rosette streamed its ribbons from Matajaca's neck. José-Ramón pulled off his hat and, waving it triumphantly, galloped twice round the ring in acknowledgement of the ovations. Matajaca went chasing after them again, much to everyone's delight, which gave Antoñio a last opportunity to flourish his cape to distract him. The memory of those mocking cheers at the beginning rankled, and with desperate courage he enticed the bull through a series of passes that would have done credit to any professional, while Señor Juan opened the gates to let Lucero and his rider out.

Everyone who could remember said that Don Ramón and Azabache had never done anything like that. Doubtless, it would be talked of for years, and without any need for embroidery or exaggeration.

11

Francisco Javier was given one of Matajaca's ribbons; Antonio and Fermín got the other two; and everyone crowded round to look at them, passing them from hand to hand with numerous comments. Francisco Javier would have been as cheerful as anyone that night except that he was still in suspense about Gavilán. He hadn't had a chance to ask José-Ramón himself, who had gone to Sevilla with the family, and Señor Juan said he didn't know which three horses the señorito intended to ask for. Neither did he have any optimistic suggestions about Gavilán's future, should José-Ramón not want him.

Why should the señorito want him, Francisco Javier asked himself, when there were so many beautiful horses on the ranch, unspoiled by Lolo's handling? He already knew that the evening's performance had had nothing to do with any personal interest in Gavilán. But what would he do if Gavilán wasn't chosen? Stay behind to look after him, or go with José-Ramón and try to forget him?

He couldn't possibly sleep with such thoughts on his mind and instead, after supper, he sat on Gaviota's manger and talked to her, remembering that she had faced the bulls many a time in her younger days and wondering what she must have looked like then, perhaps as frightened as Lucero but as trusting.

'If you could only talk,' he exclaimed, 'how many things you could tell me!'

Whiling away the time, talking to Gaviota and thinking of

102

the señorito's spectacular display of horsemanship, a new ambition was born in Francisco Javier. Pepe and José-Ramón; the bulls; Gaviota, Lucero and Gavilán; even the legendary Señorita Angeles, dead for many a year; all worked on his imagination until suddenly he knew what he was going to be, and he almost fell off Gaviota's manger with surprise.

He would be a rejoneador, like the Señorita Angeles who had travelled as far as Mexico and Peru with Gaviota. The other side of the world! He would go there with Gavilán. He saw himself galloping round the ring with the chestnut colt, receiving the ovations of thousands of people who would crowd round him as they had crowded round José-Ramón that evening – all anxious to touch and talk to him and thereby share a little of his triumph – and he would be admired and rich and famous.

With such dreams he fell asleep and didn't even stir at the noisy return of the revellers just before dawn. When he woke up, stiff and cold and nuzzled to life by Gaviota's hungry lips, his decision was the first thing he thought of, and it was like waking to a completely new life, full of hope and possibilities. He was no longer a nobody, the last monkey, because he was the rejoneador, Francisco Javier, and it didn't matter a bit whether anyone else recognized him or not. He could pity all the people who saw only Paco the stable boy. One day they'd be glad to remember they had known him.

José-Ramón chose Gavilán, along with Gaviota and Princesa. Francisco Javier was quite sure he didn't want Gaviota, and perhaps not even Gavilán, because in the days that followed he showed no particular interest in either of them. He was left with the choice of believing either that José-Ramón had chosen the horses for his sake, to give him no excuse for not going to the new place – a flattering idea –

103

or to show Don Ramón how disdainfully he felt towards the whole incident, snubbing father and brother together. Whatever the reason, José-Ramón had got what he wanted in all respects, including Francisco Javier's unreserved admiration and loyalty.

Francisco Javier would have been happier than at any time in his life except that Gaviota was daily more spiritless and uninterested in what was going on all around. She wouldn't leave the patio, spending much of the time beside the water trough, resting her chin on its edge to doze, and in spite of his trying hard to rub a shine into her skin, she looked brittle and dull and suddenly very old.

Several times a day Don Ramón stopped to talk to her affectionately and once he attacked Francisco Javier very angrily because he'd left her alone for a couple of hours. 'She comes first, remember,' he shouted. 'You're only here because of her, no matter what you might think. So stay around.'

He did stay around, impatient sometimes because he would rather have been watching Gavilán, but caring enough for Gaviota to feel guilty for his impatience. To make up for it, he brought her titbits from the kitchen and went as far as the river to cut the greenest grass he could find for her, but even her appetite was succumbing to her all-pervading weariness. This hurt him most of all. Gaviota's main pleasure had been eating. If she didn't want to eat it must mean she didn't want to live.

She was in pain and wouldn't lie down any more at night. Señor Juan said this was a bad sign, that she was probably scared she couldn't get up, so Francisco Javier slept with her to keep her from being afraid.

But he couldn't help being relieved when José-Ramón said he and his sister would require his services for the whole day, on a visit to the estate he was to take over. They would leave early in the morning before the heat became unbearable and return in the evening when it had cooled. 'But you'd better wear your hat, anyway,' he warned with a smile. 'It's a long ride under the sun.'

Señor Juan said he would keep an eye on Gaviota, and Francisco Javier was only too glad to escape her for a while, depressed by her weariness, wearied himself by so much inactivity. On horseback again for the first time in weeks, reunited with Mosca who was much livelier in open country than in the tentadero, he let fly from his head all thoughts of Gaviota and even Gavilán, intoxicated by space and freedom.

They crossed yellowing grasslands where bulls and horses grazed almost without the limitation of fences; skirted great fields of barley ripening to golden brown, and he would unthinkingly have urged the willing Mosca at a full gallop all the way, on the heels of Lucero and Nevado, except that these two were eventually checked. By the time they had passed through the gorse-covered stony hills that separated the two estates he was beginning to feel the combined effects of heat and sun-glare, dust and movement, and wasn't sorry when the ride was over.

The house was much smaller than Don Ramón's, a primitive grange whose air of neglect was not entirely concealed by the flowers cascading from pots round the walls or the canvas awning shading one corner of the patio, beneath which three small children played around the chairs and table. The occupants – Don Ramón's bailiff, the plump, smug-looking Señor Alfredo, at least twice the señorito's age; his wife Josefa, equally plump and not much younger; and her spinster aunt who waited on them – greeted the visitors with effusion.

As José-Ramón had anticipated, there was no one to look after the horses. The stable, stretching almost the length of one side of the house, was inhabited by Señora Josefa's hens and rabbits. There were rings and rusty chains still dangling

105

from the mangers, but no partitions, and it reminded Francisco Javier of the place in Sevilla where he and Pepe had worked.

One of the bailiff's children showed him the big, circular trough behind the house, agreeably shaded by tall eucalyptus trees, where he watered the horses. He drank there himself and splashed the heat and dust from his face while the three animals unhurriedly satisfied their thirst. Then he took them back to the stable, which was spacious and comparatively cool, and laughed to see how both horses and hens were startled by each other's company.

Next door to the stable was the kitchen, where Señora Josefa and her aunt rushed about preparing food.

'I'll give you something to eat in a minute,' she cried, catching him in the act of stuffing some cheese into his mouth. 'Now, out of here before I box your ears.'

With nothing to do after an enormous breakfast of cheese, sausage, olives and fruit, he decided to explore the rooms above the stable. The first, and smallest, contained lengths of sausages, hocks of cured ham and strings of red peppers turning to dust. The second would have been even less interesting but for the two torn and faded posters sticking out from beneath a pile of rags and broken chairs in one corner. They attracted his attention because he saw that they were bullfight posters.

When he had shaken off the dust and put them together on the floor, he found himself looking at an artist's colourful impression of a dapple-grey horse being attacked in the flank by a huge red and white bull, into whose gory, beribboned shoulders the rider was plunging a spear. The second was similar, except that this time a black bull was attacking from the front, while the rider leaned from the saddle with a banderilla* in each hand, aimed over the bull's horns.

* a barbed stick, 30 inches long

106

He couldn't read any of the words but he had no doubt that he was looking at Gaviota and the Señorita Angeles. Even if the dapple-grey didn't look exactly like the old mare he knew, he recognized the rider because of her likeness to Mari-Angeles and José-Ramón. In one picture she wore the typical Andalusian short jacket and trousers. In the other she was fancifully dressed in a long, green jacket with gold trimmings, white breeches and knee-length black boots.

Excitedly he smoothed his hands over the torn pieces, trying to flatten out the creases, and he gazed at them for a long time, his mind crowded with images of Lucero and José-Ramón, of Gaviota in her prime, of himself with Gavilán, of Matajaca charging and turning with death in his horns.

When José-Ramón and Mari-Angeles returned from riding over the estate he showed them the posters. José-Ramón read out the words and explained that the showy green costume was that of the Portuguese cavaliers who considered themselves masters of the art of rejoneo.

'Your aunt wasn't Portuguese.'

'No, but she learned most of her art in Portugal, where she ranked among the best even though she was Spanish, and a woman. Rejoneo isn't much practised here – it's only appreciated by those who understand it – so the Portuguese don't really have any competition from us.'

After a long siesta, made imperative by the combination of the afternoon's heat and a tremendous, four-course meal, Francisco Javier prepared the horses for the ride home. They returned a different way, through the village, where José-Ramón talked to officials about the labour needed for the fields.

Their arrival aroused a great deal of curiosity, but it was hostile curiosity. People followed them to the plaza, as far as the mayor's office, and Francisco Javier recognized them as of the kind he had lived among until he had run away to seek his fortune. They were faces without hope of people too poor even to dream. He was glad to get away from them, not wanting to be stirred by memories he would rather forget.

As Don Ramón's house came into sight all the horses automatically quickened their pace without any urging from their riders. Francisco Javier thought eagerly of Gavilán, who would pretend not to care at the sight of him but would keep an ear turned in his direction and thus betray himself, and he wondered if Gaviota had missed him very much. He had the posters tucked inside his shirt, not wanting to part with them.

Hardly had they clattered into the patio when Señor Juan came to tell them that Gaviota was dead. Francisco Javier couldn't believe it until he saw her for himself – neck stretched out, suddenly very thin-looking; eyes he couldn't recognize turned to glass without any reflection.

'It's not long since she died,' Señor Juan said. 'It seemed like she lost heart all of a sudden. She's been lying here all day, waiting – whether for death, or the boy's return, or both, I don't know. But she wasn't alone. Don Ramón was with her up to the last minute.'

While they spoke Francisco Javier got down on his knees to stroke her for the last time, bitterly regretting having left her all day, having been glad to get away from her, but her coldness made him shudder and he drew back. This wasn't Gaviota any more. It was just an old, dead horse. Gaviota – symbol of trust and courage and love – was in his heart and memory and would be there long after her body had turned to dust.

She was buried with great formality among the trees behind the house, her lifeless body dragged there by three mules harnessed in all their finery. Don Ramón talked of commissioning a statuette in stone or bronze of Gaviota and his sister with a bull. Everyone thought it was a good idea

108

but only Don Ramón and Francisco Javier felt any genuine sorrow at Gaviota's death; the one because he was burying the last memory of a time gone by, the other because he had yet again lost something he cared for.

Francisco Javier's first night at the farmstead was dismal. Without his realizing it, Don Ramón's house had taken hold of him. It had accepted and digested him with generous indifference, offered him its scraps, let him into its secrets, involved him in its immense heartbeat. It was the nearest thing to security he had ever known and, although he could have expressed none of this with words, he felt it in his heart that night, having left it all behind.

There was no warmth in this solitary farmhouse, only the crushing heat left by the sun which yet didn't disperse its innate coldness – an echo of barren lives, long forgotten. Señor Alfredo and his wife had brought no warmth with them from other places and Francisco Javier was soon to discover that they were both niggardly and pretentious.

Señor Alfredo was responsible for all the land Don Ramón had bought from his brother, Manuel, just before he was murdered, and of which this utterly neglected estate was but a third. It didn't suit either the bailiff or his wife to have José-Ramón living in the house they had, for the last three years, considered their own, and their welcome was as false as it was cordial. From the very beginning Señora Josefa showed her distrust of Francisco Javier by having all the sausages and hams hanging in the attic removed.

He was to sleep in the bigger attic, now loaded with straw and sacks of barley. A couple of cats, small and savage, had taken up residence there and he was tempted to frighten them away, not liking the way they hissed at him with flattened ears. Then he thought of the mice, and maybe even the rats that might disturb him, and changed his mind.

Princesa and Gavilán had been turned away in a long

meadow bordering the river, together with two in-foal fillies that Don Ramón had given his son at the last minute. 'Because you don't know how to take advantage of an opportunity,' he had said, referring to his choice of Gaviota and Gavilán when he could have asked for any horse on the ranch. The other horses, including Mosca, were in the stable.

Francisco Javier had believed he was going to be responsible for all of them but then José-Ramón told him he had engaged a foreman who knew as much about horses as did Señor Juan. To counter this disappointment was the news that from now on he would receive a daily wage, like any properly employed person. It wouldn't be very much because he was only a boy, and his keep had to be discounted, but the very fact that he was to get a wage at all deeply impressed him. In spite of this, he began his paid employment in debt because José-Ramón bought him some clothes which were to be deducted from his wages at so much a month.

'I don't want my horses looked after or ridden by a ragamuffin,' José-Ramón said, dumping a couple of parcels on him, 'so in future keep yourself clean and tidy. When anything needs washing or mending, you can pay Amparito to do it for you.'

Amparito was the girl who had come to help in the house because Señora Josefa said she couldn't possibly manage with only her aunt's assistance now that José-Ramón had moved in. She was about Francisco Javier's age, hardened already by half a lifetime of responsibility and work. She had looked after her four younger brothers and sisters until she was old enough to go into service and her wages were collected by her mother each pay day. Any extras she could pick up, by washing or mending, she kept for herself.

Like her mother, she was scrawny and plain, and she never had a good word for Francisco Javier, with whom she

110

shared meals in the kitchen. She started off their relationship with the remark, 'You stink!' the first time he sat down at the table with her.

'You do,' she insisted when he looked at her angrily, not knowing how to reply, even embarrassed at having to eat with a girl – something he had never done before. 'You stink of horses and I don't intend to eat every meal with the stink of horses under my nose. It's bad enough having them next door.'

Francisco Javier grabbed his plate and went off in a huff to eat in the patio. Later she brought him some peaches and said, 'I wouldn't mind eating with you if you washed first,' but he ignored her, and the fruit, still offended.

After José-Ramón had brought him the clothes and said he was to receive a wage, his dignity was sufficiently restored for him to stroll nonchalantly into the kitchen in new shirt, brown corduroy trousers and canvas shoes, and his hair plastered down with eau-de-cologne he had sneaked from a shelf in the kitchen. Amparito still laughed at him and said that now he stank of geranium flowers, but this time he didn't care. He sat down with his best imitation of Lolo at his most arrogant and demanded his dinner.

Amparito plied him with questions about himself and José-Ramón. Already wary of her tongue, he didn't have the courage to tell her his name was Francisco Javier, when she already called him Paco. And, anyway, it no longer seemed so important to insist on his proper name. No one had used it since Pepe.

Knowing that his answers would eventually be related to all and sundry he became very eloquent, without strict regard for truth. He enlarged on his adventures with Pepe – who became an actual torero, if only a novice – and he told her that the señorito was teaching him to be a rejoneador. He even showed her the posters of Angeles Casares and Gaviota, and Matajaca's rosette, and was provoked by her

111

refusal to be impressed to add that José-Ramón himself was almost as famous as his aunt in the bullrings of Portugal.

'How can he be, with only one arm?' she said scornfully. 'He can't even peel an orange.'

'Fighting bulls isn't peeling oranges,' was his disgusted reply.

'Fighting bulls on horseback is. A real torero stands on his own feet and risks his own life, not his horse's.'

'What do you know about it?' he said furiously.

Somehow Amparito always seemed to get the better of him, or at least manage to score where it hurt most. She was certainly determined to destroy his image of José-Ramón.

'How did he lose his arm, anyway, and get that ugly face?'

He didn't have the faintest idea but he wasn't going to let her know that, so he invented a heroic tale in which José-Ramón had fought off a whole squadron almost single-handed, giving his own side time to blow up a bridge to keep the enemy from crossing the river.

'And he got blown up too, I suppose?' she laughed.

'It's not funny.'

'And who do you suppose the enemy was, the people he was killing? Men like my father, and maybe yours. You're too stupid to think of that.'

Once again she had left him speechless, miserable too, reminding him of the hostility he had felt in the village, directed towards the person he most cared for. He told himself he didn't care a hoot for Amparito's opinions. She was only a girl and she wasn't even pretty. What did she know about anything?

Every day Francisco Javier took the horses down by the river a ration of barley and chaff. Gavilán would come cantering towards him just as soon as he called his name, and there was no suspicion or fear in him as he snuffled the boy's

112

hands and pockets in search of titbits or stood with eyes half closed to have his ears pulled and his jaw scratched. There were times when he was as quiet as old Gaviota, and he never left the gate until Francisco Javier had disappeared from view.

Freedom was doing him good. He was filling out again and looking proud and high-spirited.

'I'll give him three months to forget,' said José-Ramón, 'and then see what can be done with him.'

'Suppose he's just as bad then?' Francisco Javier asked, knowing that horses have very long memories.

'Then I'll sell him to the gypsies.'

Whether he meant this seriously, Francisco Javier couldn't tell, but it worried him enough to give him bad dreams sometimes. He knew José-Ramón liked to tease him, so it was as well not to ask what he really intended. The señorito was less reserved towards him now and more relaxed since he had left his family. However, Señor Alfredo's irritating servility, which only thinly disguised his hostility, made for an impossible relationship and if José-Ramón felt like talking there was only Francisco Javier to turn to.

It was horse talk most of the time, from which Francisco Javier learned a great deal, but in the evenings José-Ramón sat politely in the patio with Señor Alfredo, smoking one of the bailiff's expensive cigars, and almost completely silent while the other talked enough for both of them.

Getting the much neglected estate together took up a great deal of José-Ramón's time and energy but, whatever else he did, the horses came first. His day started at six with the schooling and exercising of Lucero and Nevado, meaning that Francisco Javier had to be up even earlier to have them ready. He learned a lot just watching this master horseman working his already highly-schooled mounts and, above all, was struck by the ease with which they responded, as if requiring no guidance beyond the very lightest reminders.

Breakfast was at ten and for an hour before this José-Ramón made Francisco Javier work hard with Mosca, watching him critically and being less patient with him than he ever was with the horses. Nothing was ever Mosca's fault, only his own.

Every evening he practised with Mosca, driven as much by his own ambition as by the fear that José-Ramón might decide he was too slow and stupid to bother with. Hour after hour they worked together and he could feel the difference in Mosca as his riding improved.

He took great care of the small, dapple grey horse. Mosca would never be as beautiful as Lucero or Nevado but whatever grooming, polishing and small attentions could achieve Mosca benefited from. He responded with growing affection and a willingness to please that made all the different to their working relationship. Instead of just obeying from habit, he wanted to do well. He was as long-suffering as he was willing and reacted to José-Ramón's favourite order – Again! – with less reluctance than his rider.

'That horse is listening to you at last,' commented the señorito one evening. 'You're beginning to use a language he can understand.'

This was the highest praise he had given so far.

12

By the end of summer Francisco Javier had all but grown out of his new clothes. Amparito made them last, adding bits here and there with an ingenuity born of necessity, taking charge of him as if he were one of the brothers she no longer looked after. She sneaked titbits for him, found remedies for his ailments, and tyrannously gave him orders. Thanks to her, his uncared-for, urchin look disappeared, and he got out of the habit of eating as though every meal was his last. However, she did everything so ungraciously, sharp with scorn and ridicule, that he could never decide whether he liked her or not and was generally glad to escape from her company to that of Alonso, the foreman.

Alonso had arrived with a cartload of tatty furniture, two dark-eyed daughters younger than Amparito, and a pale, hollow-cheeked look that only a long prison sentence gave to a man. It was soon common knowledge that he had worked all his life for Don Ramón, had been sacked by him, and had then been involved in the slaughter of his horses and bulls.

Alonso had most people's sympathy, though he refused to comment on the past, but Francisco Javier wasn't the only one left to wonder why José-Ramón had given him the most responsible job on the estate. True, there was nothing he didn't know about horses. He could shoe, geld and brand them, file their teeth, treat most of their ills, deliver difficult foals and ride with the confidence of a man who has spent much of his life in the saddle.

One day an incredulous Don Ramón came to see if the rumour that had reached his ears were true, and he almost choked with rage when nothing he said could persuade his son to get rid of Alonso.

'He's the best man with horses I know, and the past is paid for,' was José-Ramón's argument.

Señor Alfredo had been trapped into openly siding with Don Ramón, which didn't endear him to José-Ramón, but the villagers lost some of their hostility towards the señorito. Amparito, with her relentless cynicism, said that this had probably been his intention all along.

Alonso lived in the little cottage behind the house, where Francisco Javier was usually to be found every night after supper – on a chair outside the door, enjoying the freshness of the air, scented with eucalyptus, and the tales the foreman told of his days as a herdsman – while Amparito rounded up all the children and made them sing and dance together with her usual, sharp-tongued energy.

The foreman was some twenty years younger than Señor Juan, who had taught him most of what he knew, and he had a way with words that brought to life the dangers of herding bulls, the excitement of the bravery tests, the sheer hard work of the brandings. Although he was discreet about his relationship with the Casares family – he had been born in Don Ramón's house – he gave the impression that he had shared, or covered up, a lot of the juvenile escapades of José-Ramón and his brother Eduardo.

From time to time José-Ramón found his way over to Alonso's cottage, needing a break from Señor Alfredo's pompous monologues. He would pull up a chair, after asking permission to join them, and relax his characteristic remoteness to show he had a sense of humour as keen as anyone else's.

Francisco Javier could hardly believe it when José-Ramón announced that he'd gone about as far as he could with Mosca. 'I'm going to put you on Lucero and we'll see what he can teach you.' Before the boy could recover from his surprise he added warningly, 'But don't ever get the idea you can ride him without permission or you'll wish you'd never been born.'

With Lucero began the more advanced work on two tracks which the gelding could perform to perfection but about which Francisco Javier knew nothing, except as an observer. Lucero made the exacting exercises so effortless, responding almost magically to every demand, that his self-confidence soared.

'Don't forget that Lucero is doing most of the work,' José-Ramón reminded him one day with habitual disparagement. 'He's too good for you and lets you think you're doing it all by yourself. Practise with Mosca. If you've learnt anything at all with Lucero, you should be able to teach him a thing or two.'

Far more effort was involved in persuading Mosca to bend smoothly round his inside leg, or to bring out his hindquarters while keeping his forehand on the track, but his sense of achievement was great when the dapple-grey finally performed these exercises to José-Ramón's satisfaction. There were faults, he said, but this time they weren't all Francisco Javier's.

Lucero played him up sometimes, not taking kindly to a novice who occasionally confused him or threw him off balance. He wasn't as long-suffering as Mosca and objected to repetitive work which required so little effort on his part. Then Francisco Javier really had to work hard to keep him from distraction or to counteract his fits of stubbornness, not always successfully. If Lucero was in a very rebellious mood only José-Ramón could get him out of it, usually by coaxing away his sourness with a more challenging exercise

117

but, occasionally – when Lucero was determined to be awkward – by the use of his spurs.

As Francisco Javier improved Lucero took less and less exception to him. He performed half-passes to perfection, taught him the feel of the pirouette, and all the time there was still the basic work of producing complete relaxation along with complete collection, with no resistance and absolute submission.

'Anyone with a bit of practice can ride half-passes and pirouettes,' said José-Ramón, still allowing his pupil no self-satisfaction. 'You show me a perfect walk one day, and the trot, and then perhaps you can call yourself a horseman.'

Alonso's skill was more fundamental than José-Ramón's. He rode with lightness and consideration but was not particularly interested in the finer requirements of equestrianism. The most he asked of a horse was that it should work hard, be obedient, courageous and free from vices.

'Classical horsemanship is purely a hobby for señoritos,' he said to Francisco Javier one evening. 'Who else would have the time for it, or the money for horses like Lucero and Nevado? Even so, except for the Señorita Angeles, I've never known anyone who can get so much out of a horse as José-Ramón. He has her power, her instinct.'

One night, with Alonso and José-Ramón talking of horses, Gaviota was mentioned. The foreman remembered her as a foal, when the Señorita Angeles had bottle-fed her because her dam had died, and he had seen her perform on several occasions at La Maestranza.

'What a rider and what a horse!' he exclaimed. 'That mare knew more about the bulls than they knew about themselves.' Somewhat carried away, he went on, 'What a pity we haven't any cattle here! That'd liven things up a bit. Do you remember . . . .'

They took it in turn to recall hair-raising incidents and accidents of days gone by, José-Ramón remembering that at

118

one time all he had thought of was following in his aunt's footsteps, until the war changed everything. Francisco Javier listened entranced. As they rambled on he could see himself with Gavilán, and he grew hot with longing to reveal his own ambition and wondered if he could dare tell them of his dreams.

Pepe was the only person he had ever shared any secrets with. What would happen if he spoke out now? The urge to do so was overpowering, but still he held back. Suddenly he jumped up with an excuse to fetch the posters of Gaviota, needing a breathing space.

What would he say? How could he put into words the pictures that filled his mind when he had time to day-dream? Thus ran his thoughts as he pulled the posters from under his mattress and presented them to Alonso, spreading the Portuguese one on the table first. Amparito had joined the pieces together with strips of paper and a paste of flour and water.

'What's it say?' exclaimed Alonso with a teasing grin.

'Don't ask him,' said José-Ramón. 'He never went to school. If he can't read his own language how's he going to understand that double-dutch?'

They were only pulling his leg but just then he was too strung up to accept it. Suddenly they had made him feel like a little kid. His opportunity was gone and it was more than he could bear.

'I can read and write my own name,' he flared in self-defence. 'I shan't need more than that.'

He looked like a little angry bull, painfully surprised at the first feel of steel in his shoulders but standing up to it with true spirit. But it was the second prick that counted, and José-Ramón provoked him again.

'And what will you need that for? The horses won't ask for any signatures.'

Pride made him reckless. 'Toreros have to sign contracts,

119

don't they?'

'And you're going to be a torero!' José-Ramón exclaimed.

'I'm going to be a rejoneador and if they have to sign contracts, too, I'll be able to. And I'll be able to read my name on the posters. What else shall I need?'

By the tone of his voice and the impassioned look in his eyes there was no doubting his sincerity or his faith, but he was almost in tears because he thought José-Ramón was laughing at him. Alonso was the one to dash his dreams, however.

He said, 'As an apprentice torero you'd be lucky if you could afford to hire a cape and a costume and pay for its repair if it was ripped, so how do you suppose you could afford to buy and keep and travel with the horses you'd need as a rejoneador?'

Dreams don't have to do with reality and Alonso's practical words were like stones falling on his heart. For a while he was silent but eventually, more out of defiance than belief, he muttered savagely, 'I'll find a way,' and he ran off with his posters and his shattered dream, still holding both to his heart.

'Well,' said José-Ramón only a few days later, 'do you still intend to be a rejoneador?'

Francisco Javier couldn't decide whether he was talking seriously or not, but as it was a subject he couldn't joke about he answered in all earnestness, and not without some bravado, 'Of course I do.'

This was obviously the right answer because José-Ramón slapped him on the back and said, 'Then you'll start tonight. Alonso has found you a bull and I've got hold of some banderillas.'

'A bull!' he exclaimed, with a mental picture of Matajaca in pursuit of Lucero.

'What's the matter? Are you scared?'

'No sir! I just wondered where he was. I haven't seen him.'

'You'll see him tonight. He's not the biggest or the fastest and I don't know that he'd pass a veterinary inspection but, for a beginner, he'll do. Alonso and I will have a go at him first to show you how it's done. All right?'

Alonso would tell him nothing about the bull, or where it was being kept, and he began to think that a practical joke was to be played on him. However, José-Ramón had told him to saddle Nevado some time before supper and have Mosca tacked up, too, and until then he had to live with the mystery, hopeful, very suspicious, and not a little scared.

The banderillas were real enough, regulation length and decorated with paper frills, but the bull turned out to be one of the labourers – a tall, strong young man, armed with a straw-bottomed chair, who had played bull often enough for fun and certainly didn't mind doing it for money. Francisco Javier didn't know whether he was relieved or disappointed.

Before they began José-Ramón explained, 'The art of rejoneo, as with bullfighting on foot, is to persuade the bull to go the way you want him to. It's a game of high-speed manoeuvres which requires a cool head and a perfect sense of timing. Tonight we'll just practise getting the bull to turn a half-circle to meet you.'

It was just as well that the first horns Francisco Javier faced were only chair legs because Mosca, intrepid among bulls, was absolutely terrified of the chair. As it charged towards him he became almost uncontrollable and Francisco Javier's face was soon hot with shame and anger as he struggled to master the dapple-grey and, at the same time, nail home the banderilla – in the chair seat and not in Julio's body.

None of the horses liked the chair. Whatever they took it to be, it frightened them more than a bull. Nevado stopped

121

dead the first time, then leapt past his foe with flattened ears. Alonso's roan kept moving but trembled all over and looked as though his eyes would fall out and his ears drop off, while Mosca just ran out on the turn, determined to have nothing at all to do with so strange an object.

This practice became a regular pastime. Julio was both energetic and willing, considering it an honour to be bull and entering into the spirit of it as much as Francisco Javier used to when he played for Pepe. It was a demanding game, requiring great concentration of both horse and rider.

Although the chair was in no way as dangerous as a bull, it still had to be avoided. There was no expecting Julio to stop if Mosca couldn't dodge him. From the beginning Francisco Javier learned that even while he had to push his mount as close to the 'horns' as possible, he had also constantly to protect him from any blows which, even with a chair leg, could be damaging.

He began to realize, too, the importance of having a horse trained to absolute subjection. Faced with a real bull, and under great pressure because of the constant changes of speed and direction, only the most obedient horse could respond with instant accuracy. Mosca was no such horse. He was plucky and willing enough. Used to working with bulls, he got out of tricky situations by instinct, half the time not listening to commands at all, probably aware of his rider's uncertainty and preferring to trust to his own experience.

Francisco Javier suffered a few falls before he could persuade Mosca against his better judgement to do what was asked of him, and he also got a lot of criticism from José-Ramón. From both he learned a great deal.

Soon the señorito decided it would be better to have some real animals to practise with, and the men contracted to build a new stable block went on to construct a tentadero. Unlike Don Ramón's miniature bullring, it was a very basic structure. The arena was the same size, with just the necessary walls and barriers, gates, chutes and yards.

Don Ramón sent over four heifer calves. Their horns were shorter than their courage but sharp enough to lame a horse if not kill him, so they had to be blunted with leather sheaths before being let into the tentadero. The wild little heifers put up a tremendous struggle in the chute. When released they were angry enough to go for any moving object, undeterred by its size. They were fiery opponents and much more unpredictable than Julio with his chair.

No spears or banderillas were used on them – Don Ramón wanted them back for breeding in perfect condition – so at first Francisco Javier was armed with a stick, though later he was expected to get close enough to slap those charging shoulders with his hand.

The heifers were fast movers, quick on the turn but dangerously unbalanced. In their exuberance, they fell over very easily and sometimes got tangled up in the horse's legs. Yet again Francisco Javier learned how far he was from mastering both himself and his horse. Mosca got several bumps and showed his disapproval by fighting to take command.

One day José-Ramón yelled at him, 'If you were wearing spurs and this was for real, you'd make Mosca bleed more than the bull. For all the saints, control yourself or you'll never control your horse.'

Another day he could hardly walk because a heifer had caught his leg, dragged him from the saddle and knocked him about. Amparito laughed at him and, with her usual waspish wisdom, reminded him that all men were fools, even those who managed to fight a calf without getting tossed, or without falling off their horses. He could have forgiven her – for implying that he was a man – until she relented with withering charity, 'But you're still only a boy so maybe it's not your fault.'

13

José-Ramón accepted an invitation to stay at Don Felix's. Amparito seized on this information with delight. Somehow she knew, or imagined, all the ups and downs of the señorito's relationship with Conchita, and speculated on its eventual outcome with as much curiosity as the women at Don Ramón's. If Francisco Javier listened to her it was only because he was anxious to know when to expect the señorito back.

Gavilán had just been brought in. It was the time Francisco Javier had both looked forward to and yet dreaded for so long and he couldn't understand how José-Ramón could just go off and leave things as if they didn't matter at all.

'That's because you're stupid,' Amparito told him when he complained. 'All you care about is that stupid horse. Not everyone's as limited as you are.'

With time to spare, Francisco Javier worked as hard as he could on Gavilán, wanting him to look better than any other horse, convinced he was more beautiful than Nevado and Lucero put together and determined to have the señorito impressed by his appearance, if nothing else. Gavilán was looking more handsome than he had ever been, his eyes gentle, his ears inquisitive, his whole stance expressing an alert intelligence instead of that wary aggressiveness of old.

Francisco Javier put long plaits in his mane every day to encourage its natural wave; made his arm ache brushing out his tail morning and evening; washed and polished him; and if words and love alone could have made him beautiful, there wouldn't have been a horse anywhere in the world to outshine Gavilán.

He longed so much to ride him again and if he resisted it was only because of his sense of loyalty to José-Ramón who had placed a lot of trust in him. But it was very hard. Gavilán had been entirely his responsibility all this time. He had fed and talked to the chestnut every day, brushed the dust out of his coat, checked his hooves, watched him, loved him and dreamed of him constantly. And now he was to hand him over to José-Ramón for that most intimate contact of all, the subjection of one will to another.

He bought some lottery tickets in the hope of winning a fortune, remembering Alonso had said only señoritos could afford to be rejoneadores, and until the results were known he dreamed of being able to buy Gavilán. The tickets ended up in the kitchen stove, with Amparito laughing at him for his innocence.

José-Ramón was away for a couple of weeks, which seemed like a century to Francisco Javier. There were no lessons, no rejoneo, only a sharp anxiety about Gavilán's future that weighed heavily on him because he had very little else to think about. If Amparito were to be believed – and girls were supposed to know about these things – José-Ramón was likely to get married very soon, then go away on a long honeymoon, and Gavilán would be forgotten.

However, he brightened considerably when the very evening of his return José-Ramón came to look at Gavilán and was suitably impressed by his appearance. He talked to him and stroked his neck and Gavilán didn't seem to mind at all.

'Well, tomorrow we'll see what he can do, or what he intends to do, which may be different. But without a bit. This one is still a big baby.'

The señorito was in a very good mood but Francisco Javier felt somewhat cross with himself for having imagined that anything could make him forget the horses. It was Amparito's fault, with all her talk. He should never have listened to her.

The next day, just as soon as he was saddled, Gavilán began to get nervous. Francisco Javier talked soothingly to him but he was nervous himself and the horse knew it. He snorted and circled about as José-Ramón mounted, tensing up in anticipation of restraint, and was obviously surprised when he was given his head. This, and his rider's firm but gentle voice, had a calming effect on him. But he was bewildered and his instinctive reaction was to keep moving. His eyes looked wild and startled, he threw his head about, his gait was as indecisive as a foal's, but with no restraint and no demands to worry him he visibly began to settle down.

By the time he had completed a circle twice on each rein Francisco Javier thought he looked more relaxed in spite of his nervously twitching ears and his snorts. José-Ramón was now demanding a little more collection from him, but so subtly that Gavilán responded without realizing it. His head was steadier, his hindquarters slightly more co-ordinated and his wild look had vanished.

Francisco Javier felt a pain in his heart, appreciation of Gavilán's beauty and vitality, which struck him very deeply, mingled with the bitterness of having to surrender this powerful loveliness to someone else. Of course he was glad that Gavilán wasn't an uncontrollable hot-head but, even so, he had to struggle with his feelings as José-Ramón brought the colt back to him.

'Well, the rest did him some good,' he said, after patting the chestnut's neck and dismounting, 'but he's got everything to learn and a lot to unlearn. He needs a lot of time. He's very unsure of himself. He hasn't forgotten

126

altogether. You should be able to manage him, though.

'Me, señorito?' Francisco Javier's heart missed a beat and he coloured up with confusion, sure he hadn't understood correctly.

'Yes. He knows you better than he knows me and you'll have more time to work on him than I have. I've a couple of colts coming that I'm going to school, as well as Princesa, so let's see what you can do with Gavilán.'

Francisco Javier was speechless, hardly able to believe, afraid that it might be a joke; certain he must be dreaming and that any second he'd wake up to find José-Ramón laughing at him.

'Well, what do you say? You always talk too much until there's something important to be said and then there's no getting a word out of you!'

Francisco Javier hadn't ridden Gavilán in a long time and all he remembered was that sensation of oneness, that indescribable feeling which had set him to dream impossible dreams. However, the reality was nothing like his dreams. Lolo had impressed so strong a habit of resistance into Gavilán that even when he wasn't actively mutinous he was purposelessly unresponsive.

As soon as he mounted he felt Gavilán freeze into senseless panic. Words had little effect on him and Francisco Javier just didn't know what to do. Somehow he kept Gavilán on a circle, though the chestnut played up all the way, fighting to get away. He hadn't behaved as badly as this with the señorito, and Francisco Javier was in a confusion of distress, anger and hurt pride as he battled to make Gavilán listen to him.

For a while José-Ramón left him with the problem. Only when Francisco Javier, hot-faced and miserable, eventually brought Gavilán to an untidy halt did he severely demand, 'So what's gone wrong between you two?'

127

'He won't listen to me!'

'Have you tried listening to him?' was the accusing reply.

'He just closes up, doesn't want to know.'

'Then you must make him want to know and you won't do that by putting pressure on him. Stop making demands. Just sit easily – the way you used to before you thought you knew how to ride – and let him do the asking.'

It was good advice. Francisco Javier realized that if he hadn't been so anxious to prove how well he could manage Gavilán he wouldn't have needed it in the first place. At the second attempt he forgot José-Ramón, forgot the knowledge he had acquired with Mosca and Lucero. This was Gavilán, his dream horse. Together they were going to astound the world, and Gavilán knew it, too. He was the bravest, most beautiful and intelligent horse ever born . . . .

'All you've got to do is have faith in me,' he coaxed as the chestnut stiffly cavorted and bounced, spooking at his own shadow, neck and shoulders dark with sweat.

Gavilán began to calm down, tired of frightening himself, forgetting what he was going to be afraid of. He turned back an ear. There was unmistakable expectation in that alert movement and Francisco Javier felt a surge of triumph as he saw it.

'About time too!' he exclaimed, gently encouraging him into a firmer, straighter stride and forgetting about dreams. This was real.

José-Ramón worked out a very thorough programme for Gavilán. Sometimes he schooled the chestnut himself but generally he preferred to supervise horse and rider together, ironing out the faults of both at the same time. Francisco Javier didn't at first believe his warning that there were months of hard work ahead just to get Gavilán consistently responsive, but the many disappointments soon convinced him and, at times, almost brought him to despair.

'You're always in too much of a hurry,' José-Ramón told him. 'Find out why he resists. Does he know what you want? Can he do what you want? More important still, does he think he can do it? That horse is stiffer than a dead cat in January, so don't push him. Concentrate on building up his muscles until even the most difficult thing you ask becomes easy because he's physically capable of doing it.'

He finished with the tart reminder, 'And that means schooling, schooling, schooling, with no short cuts. There aren't any with horses. You can see the result of short cuts already.'

Eventually, though, there came a time when José-Ramón decided that Gavilán was sufficiently responsive to be tried out with the calves. It was an important and exciting occasion for Francisco Javier, whose dreams of being a rejoneador were never far away though he kept them to himself. He hardly slept the night before, wondering how Gavilán would behave, wondering still more how well he would manage him, and he felt pretty crushed the next day when the señorito said he would be doing the riding.

Gavilán was absolutely full of himself that morning and highly curious about the black heifer, hardly half his size, that bucked into the ring, shaking its sheathed horns. He always looked especially beautiful when so alert, ears constantly on the move, eyes bold and dark, black nostrils widely flared, and José-Ramón seemed to have a special way of changing any horse he rode with this eagerness, as vital as it was calm.

The horse had no sense of danger until the heifer suddenly hurtled towards him, then Francisco Javier could see the confusion expressed in his rolling eyes and wavering ears as obedience to his rider's command to go forward to meet her conflicted with his natural inclination to get out of her way. Just at the point where he seemed likely to surrender to instinct, José-Ramón took him away from her, thereby preventing his rebellion while satisfying his instinct to keep clear of danger.

This manoeuvre was repeated several times, and each time Gavilán was about to ignore his rider's command, the order was changed. Francisco Javier saw how nervousness and confusion left him as he got the feel that what his rider wanted was what he wanted, too. He was alert and eager again, full of confidence, and this was where the first lesson ended.

All the following lessons were based on the same pattern, teaching Gavilán to trust his rider rather than his instincts to the point where he would surrender instinct altogether to total obedience, whatever the situation. This could only be achieved gradually and, as Francisco Javier improved himself, he was allowed to do more and more of the work with Gavilán, but always under José-Ramón's very critical eye.

It was wonderful to feel how the chestnut responded to him, his obedience and skill growing along with his confidence and courage. He knew Gavilán wasn't frightened of the heifers, no matter how close they came or how persistently they tailed him, and the bolder Gavilán became, the bolder he felt himself. Sometimes José-Ramón accused him of being unnecessarily reckless.

'Remember,' he warned, 'Gavilán is leaving you to do the thinking and you're supposed to think with your head. Leave the heroics for those who need them to cover up their lack of skill. I'll not have the horses hurt to satisfy your vanity.'

He gave Francisco Javier a pair of spurs and told him to wear them. He was loathe to do so, remembering what the señorito had said about making Mosca bleed, remembering how Lolo had cut up Gavilán's sensitive skin. The points on the rowels were very fine. José-Ramón said the spurs would make him more careful with his heels, meaning it would be

Francisco Javier's fault if Gavilán suffered and, therefore, his responsibility to make sure that this didn't happen or to bear the shame of it if it did. It was a hard way to learn but very effective.

But it wasn't all work, and for both of them the best time was when schooling was over and Francisco Javier took Gavilán for a long ride through the hills, to let him unwind from the intense, disciplined work and to harden his legs. There was nothing either of them liked better than the feel of the wind, tempering the harshness of the sun. They followed old tracks, wandering round rocks and pine trees, or made their own, and sometimes Gavilán would stop to take in the different scents or to gaze at something far away.

They rode across the ploughed furrows before the seeds were sown, the heavy going tempering Gavilán's muscles, and when the grain had been harvested and only the stubble remained on the ground, they galloped against heat and dust, on and on, revelling in speed and endurance.

Sometimes Francisco Javier would stop to chat to the labourers while they rested their mules. They all admired Gavilán, who was looking prouder every day, but they were cautious in their friendship with his rider who was already known among them as the señorito's favourite. This didn't worry Francisco Javier much. If anything he felt flattered by their estimation of him, but when it seemed that Alonso was beginning to treat him in an offhand fashion he was both hurt and puzzled.

Whenever he talked to the foreman about Gavilán, Alonso was very curt. He would never stay to watch any of the work done with the calves and when one day Francisco Javier let slip a few words about his ambition Alonso attacked him with blank derision.

'What a dreamer!' he mocked. 'I thought you were growing up.'

'It's not just a dream,' retaliated Francisco Javier,

131

suddenly remembering how Alonso had tried to crush his hopes before. 'Why the rejoneo then? And with Gavilán.'

'When the señorito is bored the rejoneo amuses him. Once he has other things to think about he won't trouble himself with you. And you want to remember that. Perhaps Gavilán will be a good horse with bulls one day, but when that day comes the señorito will sell him to some professional for more pesetas than you could count, the same as he intends to do with the colts and Princesa.'

'You don't know that. He hasn't said so,' Francisco Javier cried angrily, refusing to see any sense in Alonso's warning because it would amount to a betrayal of faith in José-Ramón.

'And since when does the señorito tell you his plans?'

More gently he said, 'I just don't want to see you get hurt. Señoritos can be as capricious as the wind. I ought to know . . . . I can teach you all you need to know about horses, shoeing, foaling, stud work. The señorito's doing you no favour by filling your head with dancing horses.'

'Why not, if that's what I want?'

'Well, as long as you don't forget that the horses aren't yours and that you're not a señorito . . . .' He shrugged. 'Your ideas are big enough already. Don't let them run away with you.'

14

Francisco Javier had been riding Gavilán for about a year. In that time the chestnut had made unbelievable progress. It was hard now to remember that once he had been almost unrideable, although it was impossible to forget the months of patient discipline José-Ramón had forced both of them to endure until, quite suddenly, Gavilán lost his fear and found his confidence. Since then it was as if he was wanting to make up for lost time, responding eagerly to new demands, showing he was as intelligent and docile as ever his dam had been.

Francisco Javier would have been happy except that he couldn't forget Alonso's warning – partly because the foreman wouldn't let him and partly because his own common sense told him that as Gavilán became more valuable there was less and less chance that he could ever own the chestnut himself.

A year earlier he could still believe in his dream – Francisco Javier, Rejoneador – but on less optimistic occasions, and in spite of being allowed to ride the señorito's horses, he could see himself as Paco the stable boy for the rest of his life. José-Ramón was the only person who could change things for him.

At one time he would never have doubted the señorito's intentions, despite Alonso, but lately things were different. José-Ramón and Conchita had finally got married. When the honeymoon was over the señorito threw himself back into work with his usual energy, but now he had better things to do with his spare time than play about with calves – as Alonso had foretold.

The last lot of heifers had gone back to Don Ramón's pastures before the wedding and since then the yards had remained empty, with only the faintest smell of them to remind Francisco Javier of his doubts and dreams and fill his heart and mind with anxious wonderings that couldn't be voiced. The longing to dispel the uncertainty – to ask the señorito his plans for Gavilán, to find out if he still remembered how much he wanted to be a rejoneador – sunk like a pain to his very bones.

It was too sensitive a subject to be lightly mentioned, too difficult a matter to be broached without any forethought. If he were to say anything at all he had to find the right words and the right occasion. Wrongly put, his questions could be considered insolent, and although he knew José-Ramón could be generous, he also knew that he didn't encourage anyone to seek his favours. With Don Ramón or Lolo you could take a chance, but not with José-Ramón.

He was leaning glumly on the yard wall one evening, chasing the problem round like a dog trying to catch its tail – and in between imagining seeing a group of inquisitive heifers staring back at him, eyes bright, muzzles wet, silky ears pricked, little horns already menacingly sharp – when the señorito came by, riding Princesa.

'Dreaming of calves?' he remarked.

Francisco Javier's heart leapt as he turned. Perhaps now –! But José-Ramón continued, 'Well, soon you'll be seeing some.'

Princesa was already moving on so he couldn't ask any questions but later he found out from Alonso that some heifers were indeed on the way, though not for his particular benefit as he had excitedly hoped. José-Ramón was expecting a visitor.

'The illustrious and renowned cavalier, Don Jorge Sebastião Carvalho,' proclaimed Alonso, his deliberately pompous tone a pretty good imitation of Señor Alfredo.

'Who?'

'For you, translated, a rejoneador, one of the best known in Portugal, though most of the ignorant people here have never heard of him. Still, by all accounts, he's left even the few connoisseurs gasping. He started in Vigo, stopped by in Madrid and this Sunday intends to take Sevilla by the ears before going back home.'

'And why's he coming here?'

'His father was the Señorita Angeles' teacher and manager, one of the cleverest men with horses anywhere in the world. No doubt the horses need a break before the long trip home. They've been weeks on the road.'

'Then why the calves?'

Alonso shrugged. 'Pure courtesy, unless –'

Francisco Javier's hard gaze brought a serious, protective look to his face. He went on, 'I don't know for sure but I think the señorito's hoping to sell him a horse or two.'

'Why should he want ours?' cried Francisco Javier aggressively, hating Alonso just then for knowing what he felt. 'There must be just as good in Portugal.'

'But dearer. We've got some good young horses here, as well you know, and Jorge Sebastião is the best potential buyer the señorito is likely to come across.'

'He still wouldn't sell Gavilán,' insisted Francisco Javier, needing desperately to believe it.

'Who's arguing with you?'

For the first time in months Alonso was on his side. Francisco Javier knew it but it didn't help much. He had never felt so alone and desperate since Pepe died. The only way he could bear with his anxiety was by an act of faith. He had to believe in José-Ramón the same as he had to believe in God. He didn't think much about God, except when he

135

wanted something and asked Amparito which saint he should pray to – she knew every one of them – but this was too important to discuss over the kitchen table.

He stood on his own by the tentadero, looking at the moonmade shadows of that day's hoofprints in the sand. He thought of all the times José-Ramón shouted at him for doing things wrong and the times when he looked really pleased, expression not half so severe, and he told himself that if he lost faith in the señorito now he would deserve to lose Gavilán. By the same token, if he sincerely kept faith, José-Ramón couldn't possibly fail him.

His reasoning was as primitive as it was illogical – superstition and hope, all his inheritance in fact – but it made sense to him and drove away his fears.

The horses and calves arrived before the visitor, who was spending a few days at Don Ramón's house in Sevilla before coming to the estate. Francisco Javier helped unbox the six horses that were soon rolling and galloping and grazing at will in one of the harvested barley fields. One of them had an old scar running almost the length of his neck; another had a fairly recent horn wound on the haunch. They gave Francisco Javier something to think about.

Perhaps the horses were tired but Jorge Sebastião certainly wasn't. He was a man about the señorito's age who had been fighting professionally for seven years already, in South America as well as at home. His Portuguese-sounding Spanish was difficult to understand but he was so bursting with liveliness that he hardly needed words. It was impossible not to like him, which relieved Francisco Javier considerably. It was easier to be cheerful when everyone was in a festive mood.

Jorge Sebastião's idea of a rest was to play games with Don Ramón's heifers. One particular entertainment he introduced was caping them on horseback. He and José-Ramón held a cape outstretched between them at which the heifer was encouraged to charge, between the two horses. However, she couldn't be counted on to attack the cape in preference to the horses, and a good deal of uncoordinated reflex action had chaotic results at times – with one or both men unseated, a loose horse galloping about, and the angry heifer charging all and sundry while both spectators and performers were helpless with laughter.

The Portuguese was impressed by all José-Ramón's horses. Next to Lucero and Nevado, Gavilán was his favourite. The first time he tried the chestnut, demanding a number of changes at varying speeds in just a few minutes, Francisco Javier's pride in Gavilán overrode his anxiety. Even though Gavilán was unused to his rider, and greatly excited by the pressure put on him, he responded unfalteringly. Francisco Javier knew he hadn't done all the work with Gavilán but he had done most of it, and if ever he needed proof of his achievement with a once impossible horse he had it now, as he watched Gavilán perform so willingly with a stranger in the saddle.

Jorge Sebastião generously congratulated him but his preference for Gavilán, and their harmonious relationship, soon brought all Francisco Javier's fears to the surface and made him long for the Portuguese to leave. He fought desperately against himself – not for one second could he afford to doubt – but there was no getting away from the fact that Don Jorge was very much taken with Gavilán, to the extent that Francisco Javier never got a chance to ride him.

Alonso made matters worse, telling him Don Jorge definitely intended taking one of the horses with him. He was after Lucero or Gavilán but, as far as he knew, the señorito hadn't reached any agreement with him.

'He won't sell Gavilán,' Francisco Javier hotly insisted, unaware of the burning desperation in his eyes even though he felt it so deeply in his heart.

'It's even less likely that he'll part with Lucero,' was Alonso's reply. 'Anyway, I've warned you. A lot of money is being mentioned and I can't see the señorito turning it down to suit you.'

He stared hard at the boy, then swore angrily. Until then Francisco Javier hadn't known that he cared so much.

'See sense, boy. Gavilán is a señorito's horse. He's not for the likes of you.'

'Gavilán is my horse.' He spoke very slowly. He could hardly breathe. The temptation to give up hope was breaking him in two.

Alonso gave him a despairing look, swore again, and went away.

Francisco Javier stopped watching the evening fooling around with the heifers, even though he was invited to take part. He even stopped watching the schooling in the morning and kept out of everyone's way as much as possible. He thought José-Ramón wouldn't notice, but he was wrong.

The señorito came to the stable when he was preparing the afternoon feeds and stood watching in silence while Francisco Javier, doggedly pushing straw through the chaff cutter, back towards him, pretended not to know he was there. The noise of the cutter made the silence between them painfully unnatural to Francisco Javier. Soon he was biting his lip, trying not to cry. He was sure the señorito had come to tell him about Gavilán.

At last, with some exasperation, José-Ramón exclaimed, 'What the devil's the matter with you, Paco? I'm sick of seeing you with a long face. If you've got something to complain about, now's your chance.'

Francisco Javier was silent so long, though he had stilled the machine, that José-Ramón was about to go away when at

138

last he managed to wrench out, 'I don't want you to sell Gavilán.'

'And who says I'm selling him?'

'Alonso says – '

'Alonso, eh? It seems Alonso knows more than I do.'

'You mean, it isn't true?' He turned round with a leap in his heart, forgetting the tears on his face.

'Don Jorge wants him. I haven't made up my mind.'

His tone was as inscrutable as his expression. Francisco Javier didn't know how he could stand there so coldly when surely he must know that he himself was feeling as chopped up as the straw. He went on, 'Don Jorge could do a lot with him. You've seen for yourself.'

'But . . . .' Francisco Javier stopped. There just weren't any words.

'And you? What would you do with him?'

There was as much challenge in those words as José-Ramón had ever given him in the past, and his blood suddenly ran hot in response to them.

'I want to be a rejoneador, too, and I could do as much with him as Jorge Sebastião. No. More,' he added defiantly.

José-Ramón looked quite surprised. He pursed his lips thoughtfully then said, 'But why do you want to be a rejoneador?'

Was he teasing, or did he really think it was a stupid idea, a childish dream not yet grown out of? That's what he made it seem, just like Alonso. Either way, although he wanted to answer him seriously, Francisco Javier couldn't think what to say. How could he tell the señorito it was just something he knew? He screwed up his brow, very much aware of the grey eyes appraisingly upon him.

Once it was because he wanted to be rich and famous, to see his name proclaimed on posters in large black letters that even he could read, but that wasn't the important part

139

any more. Perhaps that bit had been only the dream, the same as he dreamed about winning the lottery. It wasn't even bull fever, like Pepe's. He shook his head, impatient with himself.

All that came to him was the memory of the evening when José-Ramón had faced Matajaca with such calculated disregard, and how deeply both his skill and Lucero's implicit trust had impressed him. It was this that had inspired him. He could imagine no greater achievement than being able to trust both himself and Gavilán with equal resolution.

But although he understood all he felt, it was impossible to put into words, however hard he tried. The nearest he could get was the impulsive but genuine exclamation, 'Because I want to be like you.'

'I suppose I should take that as a compliment,' returned José-Ramón after a pause, when his suddenly coldly scrutinizing glance had warmed to the boy's obvious sincerity. 'But I am not a rejoneador.'

'You would have been,' cried Francisco Javier, abandoning all caution now that his soul was bared. 'You could still be if you wanted to.'

José-Ramón gave a scornful laugh.

'But what you did with Lucero – '

'Was one of the stupidest things I have ever done. Perhaps I didn't have much choice. I talked myself into it.'

'But you weren't scared.'

'Like hell I wasn't. I don't know how I even managed to get into the saddle.'

In the face of Francisco Javier's bewilderment he went on. 'Look, what I did that day wasn't rejoneo. How can I explain . . . ? Rejoneo is an art form, the last word in classical horsemanship. That –' he waved his hand contemptuously, 'was suicide. I was showing off. I wasn't thinking of Lucero. I risked his life for my own pride. Any rejoneador who does

140

that is going to lose a lot of horses. It may have looked good but I was doing it for the wrong reasons.' After a pause he added, 'You still haven't told me yours.'

Francisco Javier felt his heart tightening again. José-Ramón hadn't understood! How could he make him? Why did he always run out of words when he needed them most? Amparito was right. He was too stupid for anything and because of it he was going to lose Gavilán.

Desperately, miserably, he exclaimed, 'I only know I want to be a rejoneador because I want to be like you with Lucero. I want Gavilán to be like Gaviota. I want all the world to know how brave and beautiful and clever he is. I want him to trust me. I want . . . .'

He broke off. José-Ramón was laughing at him.

'All right, all right.' He held up his hand as if to ward off any more words. 'You've convinced me, maybe just because you're in such a muddle. But I have to be sure that I won't be giving my time and my horses to someone who only wants to show what a fine, brave fellow he is.'

'You mean, I will be a rejoneador?' It was like the moon falling out of the sky.

'I mean I'll go on trying to make a horseman of you and if one day I think you're good enough I might find some bullring manager who can be persuaded to stick you on a programme and risk money on a bull for you. After that you're on your own. It's like with a guitar. Anyone can strike chords. Only an artist can make music.'

'And Gavilán?'

'It looks as if you'll be needing him, along with Princesa and the colts. Jorge Sebastião will have to find his horses somewhere else.'

It was all too much for Francisco Javier. He felt suddenly tired out, stupefied, confused . . . . He didn't know what he felt except that for some strange reason it was very painful.

'I don't know what to say, señorito . . . .'

141

'You never do,' José-Ramón grinned at him. He nodded in the direction of the chaff cutter. 'Just get on with your job. The horses are hungry.'

He stood for a moment in thought then went on, 'As you seem to have such a high opinion of yourself, how about showing us what you can do with Gavilán?'

In reply to Francisco Javier's questioning look he said, 'Don Jorge has promised my father a show before he goes back to Portugal. We're going over there tomorrow. I'll talk to him and see if I can persuade him to let you plant a few spears.'

With this he was gone and afterwards Francisco Javier didn't know if he had been dreaming or not. He went back to chopping up the straw with a mixture of such high spirits and bewilderment that he almost sliced off his finger tips. That shook him and brought him back to earth. But nothing could stop the song in his heart and the hundred thoughts that rushed through his head as he went to each horse with a ration of barley and chaff, hardly noticing what he was doing.

Jorge Sebastião's best horse, the black Lusitano, was brought up from the pasture especially for the next day's performance. Just as Francisco Javier finished grooming him the Portuguese came to have a look at him. He kissed him on the muzzle and said a few love words to him in his own language, then he gave Francisco Javier a grin and said, 'Your boss has told me that you're going to be my partner tomorrow.'

'Yes sir!'

The fervour in those two words made Don Jorge laugh. 'Will you be scared?' he asked.

Francisco Javier remembered Matajaca. He couldn't really believe that Don Ramón would sacrifice one of his bulls but anything was possible when he was feeling splendid. Honesty forced him to nod reluctantly.

'Good,' said Don Jorge. 'Maybe like that you won't do anything crazy.' Warningly he added, 'But you only do what I tell you, eh? It's my show so I make the decisions. Right?'

Francisco Javier's throat was suddenly too dry for words. The Portuguese laughed at his expression and left him alone with his thoughts.

15

It was strange, coming back to Don Ramón's house riding Gavilán. If the chestnut had any bad memories of the place he didn't show it, raising his voice as loud as Nevado and the Lusitano in answer to the challenges and greetings from the horses already there. All the time, amid the noisy welcome and bustle, the clatterings and neighs, Francisco Javier could hardly shake off the feeling that had overcome him – that all this was a dream such as he might have dreamt lying on the old mattress in the feedhouse.

The boys crowded round him, bantering but curious, and Santiago laid claim to him as if they had always been the best of friends. Francisco Javier made no pretence of humility when he told them he was to partner Jorge Sebastião in the tentadero. They didn't know whether to believe him or not. Francisco Javier just shrugged his shoulders and said they would soon find out for themselves if he was lying. They told him there was a cow in the corrals for Don Jorge, as big as an elephant and with horns on both ends. Her name was Valiente.

Señor Juan chased them back to work and stayed to talk while Francisco Javier attended to Gavilán. He asked a lot of questions about the chestnut, obviously impressed.

'So the señorito's going to make you a rejoneador, is he?' he said. 'Well, I hope you'll be luckier than Antonio. You remember him?'

Francisco Javier's best memory of Antonio was when he

caped Matajaca with such skill and confidence, but Señor Juan told him how he had been severely gored back in the spring and had lost his nerve.

'Now he can't even look a calf in the eye.'

In the kitchen, Domitila put plenty of food on the table but Francisco Javier had lost his appetite.

'Never mind,' she consoled him. 'You'll eat tonight, when it's all over.'

She washed and starched his shirt because after the long ride it was limp and dusty, and she told him all the family news – about Mari-Angeles' engagement to a banker's son, about the three new grandchildren, about Lolo's recent argument with a lamp-post in Sevilla when he smashed up his father's car, and whatever else she could think of.

Francisco Javier escaped her impatient promptings for news and gossip when he heard that José-Ramón was looking for him. It was time to go and see Valiente and hear what the experts had to say. For a long time afterwards Francisco Javier would remember with satisfaction the look on the other boys' faces when he went off with Don Ramón and all the señoritos to the corrals.

There were several heifers and a few small calves in the yards, drowsing in the midday sun, chewing the cud, but there was no mistaking the one called Valiente. She was in a yard on her own, a full grown, beautiful creature that immediately sprang to all fours at the approach of the visitors to eye them with a wild and fearless look. Her widespread horns had a slight inward curve, ending in two uptilted needle points, perfectly shaped for skewering anything within reach.

There was almost a sadness in Don Ramón's voice as he told how she came to be here, instead of grazing on the plains with the herd. She was a twin, and barren.

'Every year, when she's marked down for the slaughterhouse, I remember her record and give her another chance,' he said. 'Fourteen times she went back for punishment, and she would have taken more if we hadn't stopped her. I give her to you,' he said to Don Jorge, 'because I know you'll be worthy of her.'

Then he looked at Francisco Javier, dark eyes threatening.

'My son tells me you know what to do, and I suppose you must or Don Jorge wouldn't have agreed, but if you mess her up . . . .' He paused, trying to think of something awful enough. 'If you mess her up I'll not let you enter this tentadero again, never mind what my son says. Understood?'

Walking back to the house, José-Ramón gave Francisco Javier some advice.

'She'll go for you like an express train and she won't be stopped by a mere prick in the shoulder. So, unless you take her from the flank, both you and Gavilán will be flying over the walls before you know what's hit you. You've got to break her charges. Don't let her make a straight one. She's honest, but she knows her Latin.'

'Mathematics too,' Lolo, who was walking ahead, flung back at them. He flashed Francisco Javier a malicious grin. 'When you and that horse arrive in Pamplona you can give me a shout and I'll send someone to pick up the pieces.'

By late afternoon the number of cars parked in the growing shadows behind Don Ramón's house reminded Francisco Javier of the first time he had come to the ranch, barefoot and huddled in a blanket with Pepe. They also reminded him that Jorge Sebastião hadn't come over this Sunday on his best horse just to fool about. He might not be donning his plumed hat, his gold-braided coat and his white breeches, but in every other respect his performance was to be a professional one.

All Don Ramón's family had arrived, and the families of Don Felix and the banker, as well as friends and people from the horse and cattle clubs. Most of them knew about

146

horses and bulls, and those that didn't had read in the newspapers that Jorge Sebastião was a magician on horseback and expected to see some magic that evening.

In a stiff white shirt, and wearing a pair of leather chaps that Señor Juan had brought out from somewhere, Francisco Javier was introduced by José-Ramón to all the people who counted; and he wasn't called Paco but given his proper name. If facing Valiente was an ordeal that made Francisco Javier's stomach turn over, having to talk to these people who, under different circumstances, would have completely ignored him, was even more excruciating. In fact, he said very little beyond bravely insisting that Gavilán was the best horse in the world.

Most of the evening's entertainment was improvised, the only certainty being that Don Jorge and Francisco Javier wouldn't perform until the guests were bored with everything else. Those who didn't mind being laughed at, or who fancied being a torero, found themselves on the sand with a cape in their hands and an angry, bewildered little heifer to tease.

The smallest calves were for the children, and Don Ramón expected, and got, a lot of applause for his four-year-old grandson who arrogantly stood his ground until about the fifth time he was knocked down, when he suddenly looked like a very small boy again and began to cry. Lolo went to his rescue. Between them they chased the calf, caught her by the tail and sent her sprawling.

Everyone wanted José-Ramón to do something, so eventually he and Jorge Sebastião gave a performance they had been practising all week, caping a heifer on horseback. Don Jorge rode Don Ramón's favourite, Jubiloso, and the two white stallions with proud necks and long, flowing manes, effortlessly controlled by their riders, contrasted sharply with all that had gone before.

The men began seriously and with such artistry that the

147

atmosphere became electric – and for the first time Francisco Javier forgot his dread – but, having shown how it should be done, they then clowned through the rest, with Don Jorge riding back to front and José-Ramón making Nevado shy and shake every time the heifer came near.

But the laughter they roused didn't erase the previous emotion and, before the two men had bowed themselves and their horses out of the ring, people were beginning to shout for the real performance of the evening.

Things were already beginning to happen behind the scenes when Francisco Javier arrived. One of Don Jorge's own assistants was there, setting out everything with the earnestness of a surgeon about to perform an operation.

José-Ramón reminded Francisco Javier again about not letting Valiente make a straight charge. 'And, for all the saints, don't fall off,' was his final advice. 'That cow knows about capes and isn't likely to take any notice of them if she gets you on her horns.'

Heart thumping, mouth so dry that he couldn't lick his lips, Francisco Javier at last found himself in the tentadero, following the example of Don Jorge who was dancing the Lusitano round the ring, facing the audience, hat raised in response to the applause that had begun at their entrance.

Gavilán was excited. His black nostrils were dilated with the same fearful expectancy that made the boy's hands tremble. His ears were very stiff. He'd been dozing for most of the evening but now it was as if he knew all about Valiente behind the closed gates. He kept snorting and tossing his head.

Francisco Javier was rowdily cheered by all the boys, which brought the first stiff smile to his blanched lips, and this, together with the several exercises Gavilán and the Lusitano performed to warm them up and concentrate their attention, made some of his nervousness fade.

148

'Ready?' Don Jorge asked him as they came out of a series of graceful pirouettes. 'I'll run her for you when she comes in.'

He stationed himself in front of the bull gates while Francisco Javier cantered Gavilán over to the assistant with the spears. Everyone was silent now, waiting for Valiente.

She didn't appear. Several times the men banged on the open gates. One of them jumped down and flapped his arms towards the shadows then suddenly leapt like a maniac for safety as a black fury galloped into the sunlight and skidded to an abrupt halt where he had stood only seconds before.

Valiente did everything at full speed. Deciding she had lost the man, she saw the black horse and shot with the straightness of an arrow towards him, tail out stiff, horns half lowered because already she knew that to destroy a horse all she had to do was hook those powerful weapons of hers into its belly.

At the very last moment, and from a standstill, the Lusitano leapt away from her, and she would have crashed into the barrier had not her own reflexes been as alert as his. Within seconds she was in flat-out pursuit of him, wasting no energy hooking at shadows.

Francisco Javier was so stunned by her speed and ferocious single-mindedness that his mind was a blank. Nothing he had done with the calves had prepared him for this, or so he believed. He could have just sat on Gavilán, watching Don Jorge and the Lusitano being chased round the tentadero – as transfixed as the audience beyond the barriers – but suddenly Valiente lost the Lusitano, caught sight of Gavilán, changed tracks and cannonballed towards the chestnut, horns aimed straight at his breast.

Horse and rider had the same instantaneous reaction, to get out of her way, and now Francisco Javier knew what the señorito meant when he said even a racehorse couldn't gallop as fast as a horse with a bull on its tail. It didn't feel as though Gavilán's hooves touched the ground, but even as he became aware that this was senseless flight – and of the audience's delighted howls – he suddenly felt warm and real again, there was saliva in his mouth and his mind started to take charge.

A very sharp turn got the cow off their track. For once Valiente was deceived and went charging on after nothing. When she pulled up she was pretty sure she had chased all her enemies away. She stood high-headed and proud, front legs together, still for a moment. Don Jorge stayed unobtrusively behind her while Francisco Javier, holding the first spear, determinedly shouted her name.

There was such a silence. Time seemed to stand still between that shout, Valiente's charge, and the spectators' roar of applause as Gavilán swept along beside her, his rider trailing a flag-waving stick.

By the time he had struck home the third spear it seemed almost too easy to Francisco Javier. Valiente was so brave and true that as long as he turned her charge she couldn't get him and he couldn't miss. But Valiente was learning, too, and when she didn't respond to Gavilán's next approach it wasn't because she'd taken enough steel but because she was figuring out exactly where he was going to be. Francisco Javier wasn't doing any figuring at all, having planned his present move on her last.

He saw his mistake when she was already galloping straight into his turn, her needle-point horns only seconds away from Gavilán's flank, and it was then that the long months of disciplined training became spontaneous reaction, because there was no time to think.

The fastest pirouette Gavilán had ever performed saved them both, though the chestnut nearly lost his balance as the cow's shoulders brushed his haunches. But still he responded gallantly when Francisco Javier, incredibly clear-

150

headed, pushed him on behind her, caught up and planted the fourth spear.

After that, as far as the audience was concerned, Francisco Javier and Gavilán had proved themselves worthy assistants to Jorge Sebastião, and the Portuguese himself didn't interfere until he decided that both Gavilán and Valiente needed a break.

While someone attracted Valiente's attention with a cape, the two riders left the arena amid a storm of approval for Francisco Javier. Gavilán was steaming. All the veins in his head stood out and his nostrils showed red as he snorted breathlessly. Señor Juan threw a blanket over him and loosened his girth while Francisco Javier wrapped his arms round the chestnut's neck, feeling as though his heart would burst.

But he abandoned Gavilán to watch the next act and soon he was as baffled as the rest of the spectators by the amazing, almost unbelievable things Don Jorge did with horse and cow, including suicidally inciting her from the barrier and facing her charges at a standstill.

Valiente lived up to her name, though pitched against much fresher adversaries who mocked and goaded her without respite. Soon she was hypnotized, obliged to follow wherever the cavalier led her, his beautiful, dancing horse always just out of reach but close enough to make it seem that any second those horns must bring them down.

While Don Jorge left the tentadero to change horses, returning for the last act with Nevado, Valiente didn't move, not because she had lost her spirit – although she was very tired – but because she was utterly confused. The sight of Nevado prancing arrogantly towards her, long mane tossing, provoked her anew.

Brave to the last, she rushed upon him to be caught up in the hypnotic dance once more, drawn into an ever narrowing circle. Soon it was difficult to know which animal

151

was chasing which in this beautiful but savage ballet of black and white until suddenly Don Jorge leaned from the saddle with his last weapon – the long-bladed rejón – and thrust it from shoulder to heart.

Everyone was stunned to see that racing, three hundred and fifty kilo animal plummet to the sand like a bird hit by a stone from a catapult. It just couldn't be true. But it was because, while Don Jorge calmly half-passed Nevado round the barriers, accepting everyone's emotional applause, Valiente rolled over with her legs in the air.

Francisco Javier was pushed back into the tentadero with Gavilán to take his share of the applause. Then someone took charge of the chestnut when he was called to be praised personally by Don Ramón and his friends. José-Ramón let him listen to everyone and finally remarked that he hadn't done badly for the first time. That was enough for Francisco Javier. After what he had just seen, he knew that both he and Gavilán were still only beginners, and that soon the señorito would be shouting at him again for doing things wrong.

At a convenient moment Francisco Javier slipped away, thinking of Gavilán, wondering if he was being properly looked after. He found him in one of the yards. Someone had untacked him and haltered him to a wall ring.

Gavilán gave a whicker of pleasure when he saw Francisco Javier, and when the boy's hands went into his pockets Gavilán's eyes turned anxious with greed. Impatiently he began stamping a hoof.

Francisco Javier laughed as he pulled out the barley. 'You deserve it,' he began, 'because you're the best – '

He broke off with a gasp of pain as Gavilán's hoof came crashing down on his foot, making him drop the barley and then hop around in agony which he expressed with words even Santiago might have admired.

Gavilán had eyes only for the grain spilled over the

ground, and tried to reach it, straining against the rope.

'There's nothing more stupid than a horse,' Francisco Javier cried at him, dragging his head up angrily, 'and you're the stupidest of them all.'

Gavilán pricked his ears, blew through his nostrils and stared at him, then tried to get back to the grain.